D1824626

TWO PEAS IN A POTION

WESTERN WOODS MYSTERY #2

SAMANTHA SILVER

BERRY BOOKS PRESS

CHAPTER 1

"*T*his cannot be right. I'm totally *not* eating this."

I looked directly into the mixture bubbling away in my cauldron. It looked a little bit like someone had taken a giant mud puddle, let it evaporate for a few days, and then put it in a pot to boil. Slow, large bubbles formed, taking a few seconds to reach the surface, expand above it, and then disappeared with a long sound that reminded me of the plumbing at my old apartment which used to go on the fritz regularly.

"It looks fine," Ellie said. "Besides, I watched you do it. You did everything right and it looks exactly the way it should."

"I want to meet the first witch or wizard who came up with this potion and decided 'yeah, I'm going to put this in my mouth and see what happens,'" I muttered as I gave the side-eye to the mixture.

Ellie laughed good-naturedly as Chestnut, her little Pomeranian, ran excitedly around the table. I had lived in Western Woods for just over a week, now, and this was my first lesson in potions - or concoctology if you wanted to be fancy – taught by my roommate and fellow witch, Ellie Graham.

"It's hilarious watching you question this stuff," Ellie said. "We all learned it when we were young enough to just do what our parents said."

"Yeah, yeah, rub it in. Anyway, I'm not eating this."

"Fine, well, I guess I'm the only one who's going to feel a lot happier today."

The potion we'd been working on was a general mood booster. Supposedly, it was one of the easiest potions to master, since it only involved four ingredients – water from the ocean, mint, three hairs from a dog and a little bit of milk chocolate were the only requirements. Plus, the motions – basically the magical word for steps – were definitely on the simple side as well. Combine everything except the chocolate, rotate eight times counter-clockwise with a stick of sugarcane, drop the chocolate into the mixture, and let it sit for five minutes.

Even I, the person who in cooking class in eighth grade managed to put salt in my cookies instead of sugar, could manage that.

On the other hand, I hadn't expected the end result to look like the soup we liked to call the "mystery special" that they served in the cafeteria at lunch.

"Why don't you try some of it first?" I said to Ellie, offering her the spoon, but she grinned and shook her head.

"Sorry. I actually will take some after, to make sure it's definitely right, but part of being a witch and learning to do potions is having to test your own handiwork."

I sighed. "What if something goes horribly wrong?"

"Well, it's Heather's day off today, and she lives like three houses down from here, so I can definitely get us some help pretty quickly."

Heather Neach was the mother to Sara, another one of my roommates, and one of the witch Healers in town, which was the local name for doctors.

Taking a large, wooden spoon, I dipped it carefully in the liquid and scrunched up my nose. It wasn't that the potion smelled bad – on the contrary, I couldn't help but notice it had no smell at all – but it still *looked* absolutely vile.

I closed my eyes and stuck my tongue out, the smallest glob of the liquid touching my tongue. Ellie laughed.

"You're going to have to drink more than that if you want to see any sort of effect. But you'll notice that you're not dead, and it wasn't disgusting."

I had to admit, Ellie was right. As bad as the liquid looked, it didn't actually taste bad at all. It kind of tasted a bit like a mint Oreo milkshake. I took a deep breath and drank the rest of the liquid on the spoon, half expecting to drop dead any second.

And yet, that didn't happen. Instead, I felt a light tingling in my hands before a feeling of pure euphoria came over me.

"I did it!" I said, my smile filling my face. "I really did it! And I think it worked!"

"It certainly looks like it," Ellie laughed, grabbing the spoon off me and taking a sip herself. "Yup, it worked."

I knew that part of my happiness was simply because that was what the potion was supposed to do, but I was still genuinely happy simply from my own success. I had actually managed to make a potion, and it had gone well.

"This went so much better than the spell I did with Amy!"

"That's because potions, unlike spells, aren't coven-specific. All witches and wizards use the same recipes to make potions, regardless of their celestial affiliation."

"So until we figure out what coven I really belong to, I'll always be better at potions than spells?"

Ellie nodded. "Exactly."

"Well, I know what I'm going to focus on then. What else can we do?"

Ellie laughed. "For one thing, we can wait until I come back from work."

"Do we have to?"

"Unfortunately, yes." Ellie worked as a cook at the local coffee shop, Hexpresso Bean, and while I generally loved the fact that she could cook up the most delicious pastries and infuse them with her particular brand of magic, right now I'd rather have her here so I could keep learning.

"Ah, well. I'll come by later and say hi. I don't have much planned for today, since Sara is out doing her new job training, and Amy is at the Academy studying."

Ellie nodded. "I hope things are going well for Sara."

"Me too." Sara, unfortunately, wasn't particularly skilled at using either spells or potions. In fact, a magical mishap was the reason we now had a giant pool in the backyard. However, she was an absolute ace on a broom, and after using it to rescue me from a murderer last week, she had gone from unemployed with virtually no prospects to landing a job as a driver for a local law firm whose owners decided she could transport their elven associates to meetings far more efficiently than the current method they used, which was walking.

"Anyway, I'll see you later," Ellie said. "My shift ends at close tonight, so I'll be back around seven."

"See ya, have fun," I said with a smile as Chestnut ran out the door with Ellie. The little Pomeranian was just a ball of boundless energy.

"Good, finally that *monster* has disappeared," my familiar, Mr. Meowgi, said as he came into the kitchen.

"Chestnut is a nice dog," I scolded. "You should give him a chance."

"Right. The Trojans thought the wooden horse was a sign of peace, too."

I rolled my eyes with a smile as I placed the cauldron in the fridge. According to Ellie, this was a potion that could keep for about four days in the fridge, but would only last about twelve hours if I left it sitting outside. Eventually, the potion's powers would wile away, and while it wouldn't have any negative effects if I did eat it after the best-before date, I also wouldn't feel the same light, giddy feeling that I felt now if I did either.

"Well, I'm sure the two of you will be best of friends in no time," I said happily.

"What's wrong with you?" Mr. Meowgi asked, looking at me suspiciously.

"What?" I asked.

"You're too happy."

"There's no such thing! But, if you must know, I just successfully made a potion to increase my happiness levels." It appeared to be working, too; Mr. Meowgi's rather rude comment about me being suspiciously happy didn't affect me in the slightest.

"You witches are too naturally happy. What happened to some good old fashioned grumpiness for the sake of grumpiness?" Mr. Meowgi scowled, and I laughed. I was pretty sure that wasn't the reaction he was after.

Just then, however, my phone beeped, indicating that I'd received a text message. It was kind of funny to discover that even in the magical world, texting seemed to be the most efficient way to stay in contact with people, and cell phones were a common thing here – though because the internet didn't exist here, they were all old flip-style phones. Thirteen-year-old me would have been super jealous that I was currently flipping over a Motorola RAZR I'd been given a couple of days ago to check the text I'd just gotten from Sara.

You need to come over here, now. One of my clients just died on me.

CHAPTER 2

Ten minutes later, after I'd managed to get a bit more information out of Sara – like where the 'here' I was supposed to meet her at was – I found myself standing in front of a large, gothic-style building. This was where I'd been taken when I had first arrived in Western Woods, to see Aria King, the Chief Enforcer in town.

I could see her now, her tall frame poking up through the crowd, her golden blonde hair shining in the summer sun. Aria King was one hundred percent lion shifter, and she did not mess around.

I joined the crowd of people huddled around what appeared to be an invisible barrier – here in the paranormal world, I assumed there was no need for yellow tape when you could simply use magic instead. Paranormals of all types were pressed up against the magical barrier, like an invisible bubble they couldn't pass through, looking over the scene.

Sara's broom lay on the ground in front of the building, and next to it was a body covered in a sheet. Sara sat on the steps leading up to the court house, her head in her hands. Aria was speaking with another shifter dressed in uniform, who nodded as he listened to his boss' instructions.

I'm here I texted Sara. A minute later she took her phone from her pocket, read the message, then looked up, scanning the crowd for me. As soon as her eye caught mine, she motioned to the back of the building and got up. I took the hint and made my way around the cordoned off area, behind the building.

A minute later, Sara showed up. Her eyes were red, and her shoulders slumped. I made my way towards her, but when I got about fifteen feet away, I suddenly hit the invisible barrier and was stopped.

"There's no way past it yet," Sara explained as she saw me hit the invisible wall. "Chief Enforcer King got it to surround the whole building. But we can talk."

"Oh, Sara. Tell me what happened."

"It was awful. I was taking him – Lorondir, one of the top lawyers here – to this building. I don't know why; I never get told why. Anyway, halfway through the ride I felt him slump behind me, but I didn't really think anything of it. After all, lawyers work such ridiculously long hours, and this was one of the head honchos at the firm. I figured he just fell asleep. So I kept going, and when we got here, I went to wake him up, but he just fell on the ground. That was when I knew something was wrong. So, since Chief Enforcer King's office is right here, I ran in there to get her to help, and she called for a Healer, but by the time we got back out here he was already dead. He literally died on me, Tina."

Sobs racked Sara's body; she was obviously super shaken up.

"Wow," I said. "That's awful."

"I know. It's my third day of work and one of my bosses just died."

"Well, I guess it happens. Law is a stressful job, and hearts give out."

Sara gave me a curious look. "What are you talking about?"

"Well, my guess is he had a heart attack from the stress. I mean, it makes sense. Maybe he didn't like flying, either, and that triggered it."

"Oh God, I keep forgetting *just* how new you are to the paranormal world. Lorondir was an elf."

"So?"

"So, they're immortal. They can be murdered, but they don't have heart attacks."

My mouth dropped open as realization dawned upon me. "So he was murdered?"

Sara nodded glumly. "Yeah. While riding *my* broom."

"Is that why you're trapped in this bubble?"

Sara shook her head. "No. Aria told me I'm not allowed to leave town, but she set up the bubble as soon as she saw the dead paranormal was an elf. Anyone who was in the bubble at the time is stuck inside it until she's done her investigation, which will probably take a couple more hours."

"I'm so sorry. I bet now would be a really good time for a Hexpresso Bean coffee."

Sara nodded. "No kidding. My anxiety is just through the roof right now. I keep catching myself hyperventilating. What if Aria thinks *I* did it? I mean, he was traveling with me when he died."

"Hey, don't think about things like that. I'm sure Chief Enforcer King knows you didn't kill him." Ok, so I was lying when I said those words. After all, if anyone was going to be the number one suspect right now, it probably was Sara. She was the only person with Lorondir when he died, after all.

"She can't know that. She doesn't know me at all. She's probably over there wondering if she should arrest me for this or not."

"I don't think that's true," I lied again. "But tell me: when you saw Lorondir, did he have any markings on him? Like, was there any blood or anything?"

Sara shook her head. "No, I don't think so. Why?"

"Well, if there had been a knife sticking out of his back, or something, then at least we would know *how* he was killed," I explained. "If there were no markings on him at all, though, then it's harder. Maybe someone knocked him over the head as you rode by or something? Did you see anyone on your way?"

Sara frowned. "No, not that I can think of."

"How high were you flying?"

"We were basically floating at ground level," Sara explained. "The elves I transport don't like being high up in the air, even though Amy put a spell on my broom that makes it impossible for them to fall off it."

"That would have come in handy last week," I replied, thinking back to when I'd been knocked off my broom by a dragon who had been paid to scare me by a murdering elf.

Sara managed a smile. "She looked it up after your adventure. It turned out it came in handy given the job I had gotten. Well, handy for like, three days. They'll probably fire me, now."

"You don't know that."

"What do you think the odds are that I get to keep my job after this?" Sara wailed. "Oh, yeah, one of my bosses literally died while riding my broom, can I keep working here?"

I bit my lip to stop from laughing; it sounded a bit ridiculous. But at the same time, I knew Sara had a point. I didn't know what kind of labor relations and worker protection laws there were in the paranormal world, but I had a feeling that having your boss die on you wasn't a great way to keep your job.

"Well, what if Aria figures out who killed Lorondir?

Then there would be no way for them to deny you your job, since it wouldn't have been your fault."

"Maybe," Sara said, looking dejected. "My mom was so proud of me, too. This was the first job I'd gotten in so long, and it actually involved using magic, even if it wasn't spells or potions."

"I know. Okay, we're going to make sure that whoever did this is found, so that you get to keep your job."

"I don't know," Sara said. "What if it doesn't work? What if it's hopeless?"

"Well, it's definitely hopeless if you give up now," I replied. I knew Sara had some self-esteem issues, and I knew that she had a tendency to give up on herself too quickly, and I wasn't about to let that happen.

"Okay, fine. We'll do it. But we have to be careful. And if we figure out who it was, we have to tell Chief Enforcer King this time."

I nodded. I had absolutely no intention of repeating what had happened last time, when I was almost killed by an elf, along with Mr. Meowgi.

"So what are you going to do? I'm stuck here, for goodness knows how long."

"Find out everything you can about the murder," I ordered. "I'm going to go see Ellie, and Amy, and we'll start taking over from here."

Sara nodded, and I could see that having a plan in place was beginning to galvanize her. Her shoulders weren't quite as slumped, and the redness was leaving her eyes.

"Okay. I have to find out whatever I can from whoever I can in here. I'll meet you back at home as soon as I'm released. If I'm released."

"You will be," I said, with more confidence than I felt. As much as I knew Sara would have never killed anybody, I was also well aware that things looked really, really bad for her right now.

I flashed her a smile that I hoped exuded confidence. "It's going to be fine. I'll see you at home in a few hours, and we can see what everyone has found out."

With that, I turned and walked away, wondering what on earth I had gotten myself into again.

CHAPTER 3

*H*expresso Bean was a large, comfortable space with exposed brick walls, plenty of seating, and a constant murmur of conversation which floated up from patrons. I had only lived here a week, but I had never seen Hexpresso Bean be less than almost at capacity. Not only were all of the tables almost always taken, but there was always a lineup of paranormals standing by the coffee machine waiting for their take-out orders.

I made my way to the front counter, where I was greeted by a fairy I hadn't seen before - short, wavy brown hair reached her shoulders, framing her sparkling blue eyes that matched her fluttering wings perfectly.

"Oh, you're the new witch in town, aren't you?" the fairy asked.

I nodded with a smile. I was pretty used to this

question by now. "That's me," I replied. "I'm Tina. It's nice to meet you."

"Bluebell," she replied with an equally friendly smile. "It's nice to see some new blood in town. I feel like a lot of the paranormal towns are far too insular and we would benefit a lot from an outsider's experience."

"Well, thank you," I said with a smile. "I'm not sure I have that much to offer the town, but I do my best."

"That's all any of us can do, isn't it?" Bluebell replied. "Now, what can I get for you today?"

My eyes were drawn to the cabinet of baked goods that I knew had been infused with some of Ellie's skilled magic, and as my stomach growled I knew I wasn't going to be able to resist.

"What are these hocus-focus cupcakes?" I asked, my eyes drawn to the row of gorgeous white cakes topped with sprinkles that shimmered in the light.

"Oh, they're fantastic," Bluebell replied. "Not only do they taste amazing, but if you're doing something that requires intense concentration, they help you focus on the job at hand and avoid distractions. Back when I was at the fairy Academy, those cupcakes got me through quite a few exams."

"Sold," I replied with a smile. After all, if I was going to try and learn whatever I could about the dead elf, I figured a little bit of focus could only help. "I'll take one of those and a coffee as well."

"Sounds good," Bluebell replied. "I'll add it to the coven's tab."

Apparently, word had gotten around that I wasn't to pay for anything, but rather the coven was going to cover all of my costs until my magic reached a level that was suitable enough for me to work a job. I fully intended to pay the coven back for everything they bought me up until then.

"Thanks," I said, shooting Bluebell a grateful smile.

"Not a problem. Find yourself a seat, and I'll bring it all out to you when the coffee is ready."

"Could you ask Ellie to come out and say hi if she gets a chance?" I asked. I wanted to tell Ellie everything I'd found out from Sara as soon as possible.

"Sure thing," Bluebell nodded. "I'm pretty sure she has a break coming up, so she should be out shortly."

I took a seat in a hard backed chair at a small square table that had just been vacated by a couple of vampires. About a minute later, Ellie came sauntering out from the back, and plopped herself down on the chair across from me with a smile.

"What's going on?" she asked. "I wasn't expecting you to come in today."

I leaned in close, not wanting anybody at nearby tables to overhear. "Sara texted me a little while ago. She was driving one of her bosses and he literally died on her broom. He was an elf, so it has to be murder Sara tells me."

Ellie's eyes widened as she clamped her hands over her mouth. "You're joking."

"I wish I was. I went over there, and I spoke to Sara. She's worried about not only her job, but also being arrested. And I mean, we obviously know that Sara would never do anything to hurt anyone, but how can Chief Enforcer King know that?"

Ellie nodded. "Especially with her being a new hire and all. Oh man, this isn't good at all."

"I know. I told Sara we would do our best to find out who actually killed Lorondir."

"Did you say Lorondir? He's the one who was killed?"

I nodded. "Yeah, why?"

"He's probably the most famous lawyer in town. He has been working in Western Woods for literally thousands of years."

"Seriously?" I asked. This time it was my turn to have my eyes widen.

Ellie nodded. "Yeah. I mean, elves are immortal, and a lot of them are incredibly old. Lorondir once told me about how he used to hang out with Socrates, who was a wizard, but preferred the human world to the magical one."

"That's insane," I whispered. "But wait, how come there aren't like a trillion elves around if none of them ever die?"

"It's incredibly difficult for them to reproduce," Ellie explained. "For one thing, there are very few female elves. In all of Western Woods there are like, ten of them, and hundreds of male elves. So as a result, most elves don't end up having children. And for the ones that do, both parents have to be elves for the child to be immortal. An elf can have a child with, say, a shifter, and while the child could have all of the elfin characteristics magic-wise, they would live as long as a shifter would, but eventually die naturally."

I nodded slowly. My thoughts immediately turned to Kyran, an elf that I spoke to occasionally. I wondered how old he was; I had kind of assumed that he was about my age, since that was how old he looked, but I suddenly realized for the first time that he might have in fact been centuries, if not millennia old.

"Anyway," Ellie said, getting the conversation back on track. "What do you know about Lorondir's death?"

I shrugged. "Not too much, yet. Sara says there was no blood that she noticed on the body, so it's unlikely that someone ran up behind them and stabbed him. She also said that they drove on her broom basically at street level, since the elves don't like being high up in the air."

"So that means anybody in the street could have attacked him, as long as they did it subtly enough that Sara didn't notice." Ellie frowned. "There are a lot of problems with that theory though."

"Exactly. Like, the fact that Sara didn't remember passing anybody in town. Although, she may simply not have noticed them. Plus, it would've been a huge risk for the murderer. There would have been no guarantee that Sara would not have noticed them, and how would they have known that Lorondir was going to come by that day at that exact time?"

"I agree. Do you have any idea of what might have actually happened?"

I nodded. "I think he might've been poisoned."

Ellie nodded slowly as she thought about the words. "Yeah, that actually makes a lot of sense. If he was poisoned, then he might have ingested the poison before actually getting on the broom, and its effects may have been delayed for a little bit."

"I assume the magical world does have poisons in it?"

"Of course," Ellie replied. "We have access to most of the human world poisons, things like mushrooms that grow in the human world also grow here. Plus, witches and wizards are able to make special potions that can cause death."

"Are elves able to make potions? What about shifters?" After all, I didn't know too much about the paranormal world, and I wanted to make sure I had all of the facts before we got started. Just then, Bluebell came by and placed the coffee and cupcake down for me with a smile.

"Here you go, do you need anything else?"

"No, that's great, thanks," I replied with a smile, trying to resist digging into the cupcake with gusto. The coffee was a work of art in itself as well. Rather than a plain latte and a cup, the coffee's here came in large mugs, and looked a lot like freakshakes you'd find in the normal world. This one had rainbow colored syrup running down the side of the mug, which was filled with coffee that had a suspicious pink tinge to it, and was topped with copious amounts of pure white with cream, multicolored sprinkles, and a few different colored candy sticks on top just to finish things off.

It was a good thing that it was recommended to only have one Hexpresso Bean coffee per day; I was pretty sure my waistline wouldn't appreciate it very much if I had any more than that.

As I dug into my food and drink, Ellie answered my question.

"Shifters can't make potions at all," she replied. "If they go through the steps, nothing happens. For someone to be able to make a potion, they have to have a certain magical ability inside of them, or the magical energy doesn't transfer to the cauldron, and shifters are missing that. Their magic is different. Some elves have the ability to do it, since they do have magical powers that are similar to ours, but not all. The older and wiser the elf, the more likely they are to be able to make potions. A lot of them don't bother even trying, since if they get it wrong, it can go really wrong. Playing with potions is a real risk for elves."

"But then, so is murder," I replied. "If an elf was desperate enough to murder Lorondir, I could see them being desperate enough to try making a poisoned potion."

"That's a good point," Ellie said. "And on top of that, there is no guarantee that whoever did it didn't simply ask a witch or wizard to make that potion for them. That person, when they find out about the murder, would probably keep quiet because they wouldn't want to be implicated."

I nodded. "So if he was poisoned - and I think we should stick with that as our working theory, because it seems most likely - then it likely happened at his office sometime."

"I think so," Ellie said. "Is that where you're going to go after this?"

I took a big bite of the hocus-focus cupcake and momentarily ignored Ellie's question as I savored the sweet frosting mixed with moist cake. This was easily the best cupcake I'd ever had in my life. When I opened my eyes, I suddenly felt an intense concentration. This was definitely the focus part of the cupcake kicking in.

"Sorry," I said to Ellie, finding my voice picking up speed slightly. "I just had to savor that for a moment; that was the best cupcake I've ever eaten in my life."

Ellie grinned. "Don't ever apologize for enjoying food I've made. I love hearing about it."

"To answer your question, yes, I think visiting the law offices is probably the best way to go."

"I wish I could go with you, but I'm stuck here for a few hours still. You should text Amy though; she knows her way around the paranormal world pretty well, and you'll be more likely to get a lot of information with her around."

That was definitely a good idea. I glanced at my watch; Amy was due back from the Academy where she was taking advanced courses any second. Pulling out my phone, I sent her a quick text asking her to meet me here. That would give me a little bit of time to gather my thoughts, maybe come up with a plan, and definitely finish eating this cupcake before she got here.

"I have to head back into the kitchen, since my break is over, but let me know what the two of you find," Ellie said. She stood up, and I gave her a quick hug, promising to let her know anything we discovered before she made her way back to work.

CHAPTER 4

"You're out of your mind, you know that?"

I supposed I shouldn't have expected any other reaction from Amy. After all, Amy was basically Hermione, but in real life. A total book nerd, and an incredibly gifted witch, Amy was completely opposed to breaking the rules in any way – well, most of the time. And that definitely applied to investigating a murder when we had absolutely no official links to law enforcement.

"What other options do we have?" I asked. I had just finished explaining to Amy everything that had happened that morning, and she was definitely not on board with our plan.

"Oh, I don't know, how about leaving it for the professionals?" Amy replied sarcastically. "After all, don't you remember what happened last time? You almost died."

"I know. That's why we've decided that if we do figure out who did it, we're going straight to Chief Enforcer King. We're not going to do anything stupid this time."

Amy narrowed her eyes at me. "Do you not remember that last time you were also swept off a broom by someone the murderer had hired as well?"

"I know, but he hadn't actually meant to try to kill me," I replied. "It was an accident." After Sara and I had reported what had happened to the head shifter, Jomund came to see me and apologized, explaining that he hadn't realized that I was so new to broom riding that I wouldn't be able to stay on my broom when the wind from his dragon wings hit me.

"Killing someone by accident is still killing them," Amy said, crossing her arms.

"Fine, you don't have to come. But Sara's in trouble, and she was there for me, and I'm going to do whatever I can to be there for her now."

Amy let out a long, dramatic sigh. "And of course, I can't let you go to the offices by yourself. After all, you barely know your way around town. Do you even know where the law firm is?"

I shook my head sheepishly as I realized I probably should have asked Ellie that before she went back to work.

"All right, let's get going then," Amy said.

"Does that mean you're going to help?" I asked, trying to keep the enthusiasm out of my voice.

"It doesn't look like I have any other choice."

Ten minutes later, with my coffee drunk and my cupcake eaten, Amy and I walked down the street towards a large, wooden building. It had been painted white, with dark exposed beams accenting the sides. A large sign above the door announced that we had arrived at the Western Woods Law Offices. This was definitely where we wanted to be.

"So who needs a lawyer in the magical world, anyway?" I asked Amy. "Is it the same as in the human world?"

Amy nodded. "Yes, more or less. If someone has committed a crime, they need a criminal lawyer. If someone is looking to sue another paranormal, they need a civil lawyer."

"What type of lawyer was Lorondir?"

"He was a criminal lawyer. And in fact, he was one of the best criminal lawyers in the entire paranormal world. He was often called away to other paranormal communities and hired by their defendants for representation."

"Does that mean that paranormal laws are enacted across towns? Or does every town have its own laws?"

"While each individual community is able to create its own laws, the overriding set of laws that rule Western Woods is the same across every paranormal town. So someone who learned to become a lawyer here can practice law in any paranormal town in the world."

"So Lorondir would have definitely defended a number of murderers, right?"

"That's correct," Amy nodded. "I know there was one high-profile case a couple of years ago where Lorondir spent almost six months away. I believe he ended up losing that case, but when his client appealed with a different lawyer, the initial ruling was overturned."

My eyebrows rose. "That doesn't sound like the work of one of the world's best paranormal lawyers."

"No, and in fact I think it was one of the reasons why Lorondir was considering retirement. I know I had heard around that he was thinking about it, but evidently he hadn't gone through with it just yet."

The two of us stepped through the front doors and found ourselves in a high ceilinged reception area, with plush red carpet and a friendly-looking fairy behind a large desk looking up at us politely.

"Hello and welcome to the Western Woods Law office," the fairy told us, her pale green wings fluttering behind her. "How may I help you on this fine Wednesday morning?"

If she had heard about Lorondir's death - and at this point, how could she not have - she was hiding it very well. This fairy was definitely a professional.

"Hi," Amy said to her. "My friend here recently had an encounter with a dragon shifter, and we would like to speak with an attorney about potential damages."

The woman looked past Amy and over at me, and I

flashed her a shy smile. I could see the curiosity in her eyes, and I knew she could tell that I was the new witch in town, but that she was far too polite to mention anything.

"Of course. While I don't have anything available right at this moment, in one hour Manarwa has a slot available. You're welcome to wait here, of course, or you could come back then."

"Thank you, we'll just wait," Amy said with a smile, leading me towards a waiting area in the corner where plush, leather chairs surrounded a large, live-edge coffee table covered in magazines. It appeared that even in the paranormal world, waiting rooms were still exactly the same as back in the human world.

Amy and I sat down next to each other and a couple of chairs, and I couldn't help but notice that Amy had specifically picked chairs that gave us a perfect view of the room: we could see anybody coming in or out, and we could see what the receptionist was doing at any given moment as well. Amy also had a notepad and a piece of paper out; she evidently had come a lot more prepared than I had.

In an attempt to not look super suspicious, I flicked through the magazines, trying to look like I was just after some reading material.

Better Homes and Covens
Vampire's Digest
Elf Weekly
Vampire Fair

Shifter Living

I grabbed a copy of *Better Homes and Covens* and began flipping through it. Mostly ignoring the articles, I peeked over the top of the page and paid attention to everyone who came in and left.

Frustratingly, this law office seemed like a high turnover place. I had hoped that there would have only been five, maybe six people who would have been in here early enough to poison Lorondir, but given how many people came and went from the door behind the reception desk that seemed to lead to the offices, it appeared I had no such luck.

Amy, however, was scribbling down names as people came and went. She was obviously familiar with most of the clientele in this place. I was suddenly thankful for the fact that she had decided to come after all; she was right when she said that I would have needed her help.

"We need to find out who Lorondir saw this morning," I whispered to Amy. "After all, Sara called me just after eleven, which means that someone who was here before then has to be the poisoner."

Amy nodded. "You're right, but the fairy at the desk will never just give us that information."

"I'll try and distract her," I said, standing up and making my way to the reception desk before Amy could protest.

"Excuse me," I started, giving the fairy a polite smile. "I'm wondering if you'd happen to have any bathrooms available. I'm so sorry, but I just came from Hexpresso Bean and, well, you know how it is." I flashed her an embarrassed look, and the fairy smiled and gave me a curt nod.

"Of course we do," she said. "Please, follow me."

I winked at Amy as I followed the fairy through the doors that led into the main part of the offices. "I apologize for having to take you here myself," the fairy said. "Unfortunately, the space back here is rather maze-like, and if you don't know where you're going, it's quite easy to get lost."

"Well, I appreciate you making the time for me," I said. "I'll try to be quick."

Sure enough, I followed the fairy around a number of meandering paths, and I realized that even if I had found the bathroom by myself, I never would have found my way back to the waiting area without help. Eventually, we stopped in front of a plain wooden door, and the fairy smiled and motioned for me to enter. I went in, used the bathroom while lingering as much as I felt I possibly could, hoping that I had left enough time for Amy to find that morning's appointment list and write down all the names.

By the time we got back to the lobby, Amy was back sitting exactly where she had been when I left, not giving off any indication as to whether or not she had been successful. I thanked the fairy once again, and she took her place back at the desk, while I sat down next to Amy once more.

"So?" I asked in a quiet voice, raising my eyebrows at her.

Amy replied by handing me her notebook. On it was a list of names, most of which I didn't recognize.

"The four at the top were the people Lorondir saw before his death," Amy whispered to me. I focused on those four names in particular.

Farawir

Jordan Black

Maria Grecu

I had to admit, none of those names meant anything to me. I couldn't even tell what species of paranormal they were, except for the two elves at the top and the bottom of the list. Still, now that we had the names, we could definitely begin investigating.

"Manarwa is ready to see you now," the fairy said suddenly a moment later. "If the two of you could please follow me, I'll be happy to take you to her."

I handed Amy back her notebook and the two of us stood up, following the fairy back through the door and into the offices behind.

CHAPTER 5

*T*his time, rather than a convoluted path to get to the bathroom, we took a straightforward route down the first hallway and stopped at the third door on the right. The fairy knocked curtly twice, then opened the door for us, leading us into the office.

Manarwa's office definitely followed the décor of the rest of the place, with an old-fashioned, classy look. The carpet was the same plush dark red as in the lobby, and the client chairs in front of her large mahogany desk were identical to the ones Amy and I had waited for her in.

Sitting behind the desk was a tall, graceful elf with completely straight dark hair that hung down to her hips, flowing behind her as she stood up to greet us. Her eyes were as dark and deep as the sea, and there was an ethereal beauty to her. I had absolutely no idea how old she might have been, but as I looked along the wall, I couldn't help but notice a copy of the Magna Carta. I wondered if Manarwa had somehow been involved in its creation; it seemed like with elves, that sort of thing was a very real possibility.

"Welcome, I'm Manarwa, one of the senior elves at the firm. Elloita tells me that you have had an encounter with a shifter in its animal form during the day time," she said, looking over at me. "But I have a feeling you're not really here about that, are you?"

Great. I'd forgotten that elves had semi-psychic abilities, where they couldn't directly read thoughts, but they were super intuitive in a way that made it incredibly difficult to hide anything from them.

"We're not," Amy admitted. "Have you heard about Lorondir?"

Manarwa's gaze fell to her desk, and I knew the answer before she replied.

"Yes," she said sadly. "I heard a few moments ago. It's quite tragic. But I must ask why the two of you are here."

"We're not onlookers trying to get in on the tragedy or anything," I said quickly. "Sara, the woman who was flying Lorondir when he died, is our roommate and friend."

"Ah," Manarwa replied. "So you're here to help your friend."

"We're hoping so. While we know she's innocent from any wrongdoing, we also know that in an investigation everyone needs to be looked at, and he did die on her," I said, hoping that honesty would get us some more information from Manarwa without getting us kicked out of her office.

"Do you know how he died?" Manarwa asked. "We were not given any details, only that he passed away. Obviously, since that's not a natural occurrence for elves, we have a lot of questions."

"We suspect he was poisoned," Amy replied. "According to Sara, there were no marks on his body."

"That's a blessing, at least," Manarwa said. "On the rare occasions that an elf funeral does take place, we prefer to have open ceremonies privately among the elves before the public ash scattering ceremony. It would have been tragic if Lorondir had to be denied that due to the state of his body."

"It doesn't sound like that's going to be a problem," I said.

"And it's such a tragedy that this has happened so close to Lorondir's retirement."

"His retirement?" I asked.

"Yes, Lorondir had been practicing law for nearly four thousand years. It was high time he retired, and even though he resisted at first, I know that for the last few weeks he was looking forward to a more leisurely existence."

"What about his clients?" Amy asked.

"Well, it's been known that he was going to retire for the last six months or so. Ever since then, he has taken on far less work, to the point where I believe he only had one client left."

"Wasn't he one of the owners of the firm?" Amy continued.

Manarwa nodded. "Yes, he was. In fact, he was the largest single owner of this law firm, having started it right from the beginning two hundred years ago when Western Woods was first formed."

My eyes widened at this revelation; it was strange to think of Lorondir being *here* for literally hundreds of years.

"So what happens to his shares in the business?" Amy asked.

"Oh, that's all been taken care of," Manarwa replied. "Lorondir sold his shares to one of the other partners, Handromir, who is now the largest owner of the law firm. I believe they finalized their agreement about a week ago. Lorondir was still working, but only to finish up the one case he had left. After it ended, his plan was to retire for good. I know he earned a substantial sum of money in his lifetime, not to mention the enormous payout he got for his shares from Handromir. Lorondir was supposed to have a nice retirement, a comfortable retirement. It wasn't supposed to end like this."

Manarwa was blinking back tears now, and I averted my eyes so that she wouldn't notice that I'd seen. She was obviously trying to hide her emotions, and definitely making an effort to keep it together.

"Can you think of anybody who might have wanted to hurt Lorondir?" Amy asked softly, and I had a feeling she had noticed the same thing that I did.

Manarwa shook her head. "No, I can't. Lorondir was well-liked, he was a pillar of the elfin community, and I truly can't imagine that anyone would have wanted him dead. Of course, I can't speak for his clients. Not only would that be a breach of confidentiality, but on top of that I knew very little about them. After all, as a practitioner of civil law rather than criminal, I had very little to do with Lorondir professionally."

"What about that case from about six months ago?" I asked. "It was very high profile."

"You must be talking about the Jordan Black case," Manarwa said. "Unfortunately, I'm unable to speak about that one beyond what was reported on publicly."

"Lorondir lost that case, didn't he?" Amy asked.

Manarwa nodded. "He was incredibly upset about it, too. I'm sure he thought he was going to win. Jordan Black was a shifter, who lived in a paranormal town called Shifterfield, in England. As I'm sure you can tell from the name of the town, it's a place where the dominant paranormal species are shifters."

"Jordan Black was convicted of murdering one of his clansmen, right?" Amy asked, earning herself another nod from Manarwa.

"Yes, that's right. Jordan protested his innocence throughout, although he was eventually found guilty.

He was very angry with Lorondir, and verbally attacked him in court after the verdict was read. He fired him as his lawyer immediately, and the lawyer who took over afterwards actually had the verdict overturned. Unfortunately, I don't know the details of why or how that happened."

I mulled over this information in my head. Jordan Black had been on the list of people who had an appointment to see Lorondir that morning. Maybe he was angry enough about the representation he had received to come over and poison Lorondir.

"Did he do it?" Amy asked, leaning forward. "I know that the law says he didn't, but if a jury found him guilty, it means there must have been at least some evidence against him. Do you think Jordan Black killed his clansman? Off the record." Evidently, Amy's thinking was going the same way as mine was. After all, if Jordan really had killed that man originally, it wasn't too much of a stretch to think he'd kill again.

"Strictly hypothetically, as the courts have ruled on this issue and the reality is I do not know one way or the other, I believe Jordan Black did kill that man."

"Why did Lorondir defend him, then?" I asked. "Did he know he was a killer?"

"One of the pillars of our criminal justice system involves the right of the defendant to have a lawyer. Whether or not he was guilty of the crime, Jordan Black was still entitled to the best representation he could afford. And in his case, those were the services of

Lorondir. Jordan Black came from a powerful clan, and he had access to a significant amount of money. He hired Lorondir because that was his right, and Lorondir defended him because he knew that regardless of Jordan's innocence or guilt, he still deserved a lawyer to fight for him."

"But you think it's possibly likely that Jordan Black did commit murder in Shifterfield?" Amy asked.

Manarwa nodded. "Off the record, of course. But yes, I think it's likely he did do it. Why do you ask about him? As far as I'm aware, he went back to his life in Shifterfield."

"We heard he was in town at the moment," Amy replied, not giving away the fact that we had snuck a look at the calendar for the day.

"That's news to me," Manarwa said, raising an eyebrow. "Anyway, I do hope the real killer is found. Your friend is a nice girl; she flew me from here to visit a client yesterday. I liked her, although I don't think she realizes that her magic is significantly better than she thinks it is."

"You're absolutely right there," Amy said with a nod. "Thank you for your time, and I'm sorry about Lorondir."

"Thank you," Manarwa said softly. "It always comes to us as a shock when we lose one of our own. Lorondir was a good elf."

Amy and I got up from our seats and saw ourselves out. This had definitely been an interesting chat.

CHAPTER 6

"*D*o you think Aria knows that Jordan Black is in town?" I asked Amy as we left.

"Well, she's not totally incompetent, so the first thing she is likely going to do if it turns out it was poison is visit the office and see who Lorondir met with that morning. So yes, if she doesn't know already, I'd say she's going to know fairly shortly."

"Good, because I think it's most likely that he did it."

"He certainly had a reason to, it sounds like. I wish we knew more of the details that led to Jordan Black being convicted, and then having it overturned by another lawyer."

"Is there a way to get that information?" I asked. "Like, is there some sort of paranormal Freedom of Information Act?"

Amy nodded. "There is a way, yes. I can put in a

request, but as with any bureaucracy, it may take some time."

"Well, in the meantime, I think we have ourselves our main suspect. Do you know who the other people on the list this morning were?"

Amy pulled her notebook out and began to scan it once more. "Farawir is Lorondir's son, but I don't know much about him other than that. Maria Grecu is a vampire; I'm pretty sure she would have seen Lorondir about her upcoming court case, since she was accused of biting another vampire in a bar a couple of months ago. Apparently, she had a little bit too much to drink."

"Is that a crime, to bite another vampire?"

Amy nodded. "Absolutely. It's a much more serious crime to bite a human, of course, but even biting another vampire is considered to be one of the most stringent assaults a vampire can commit against another vampire. They take it extremely seriously, and Maria is facing potential punishment of five years in prison for it."

My mouth dropped open. "Wow! That's a long time to spend in jail for biting somebody."

"Yeah, it is. I know they've let her out on bail until her trial begins, so she's around. She's just not allowed to consume any alcohol, and they made her take a potion that one of the witches made which will alert Chief Enforcer King if she has any sort of alcohol intake."

"So she's not likely to have a beef with Lorondir. Not yet, anyway, since her trial hasn't started yet."

"Exactly."

Before we got a chance to decide what to do next, I got a text from Sara.

I'm finally out. I'm heading home; can you grab something for dinner? Don't really feel like cooking tonight.

I relayed the message on to Amy, who nodded and suggested we stop at Two Wizards and a Griddle.

"Lead on, I have no idea where that is, but it has the word griddle in it and that's enough for me," I said.

Amy led me to a small, single-story cottage that had been painted a kind of pastel red color. The dark wood accents on the outside really made it fit in with the rest of the town, and a small sign above with the picture of waffles was enough to let me know that we were in the right place. Waffles were always a good sign.

To my surprise, the inside of the diner was decorated exactly like a 50s style American one. It was like stepping back in time, complete with Frank Sinatra music coming from a real jukebox.

A fairy in a polka dot dress made her way over with a couple of menus.

"Table for two?" she asked, looking down at the mostly empty tables. Seeing as it was now just two in the afternoon, we were too late for the lunch rush and too early for the dinner rush, so there were only a couple of tables occupied by an elderly witch and wizard, and another where three teenage shifters were obviously playing hooky from school. Given the furtive glances they kept giving us, I had a feeling this was a first-time experience for them.

"We're just going to order take-out, if that's alright," Amy said with a smile.

"Of course. You're welcome to have a seat, look at the menus, and I'll come by in a minute to take your orders."

As soon as I began looking through the menu, even though I had recently finished what had to be a pretty calorie intensive coffee and a very rich cupcake, my mouth began to water. This was true, traditional diner food at its finest. All-day breakfast, twelve different burger options, and more.

I had a feeling this place was definitely going to become a regular habit for me.

Twenty minutes later, Amy and I left the diner, arms laden with bags full of burgers and enough curly fries to last a week.

"This would have been a lot easier if we had brought our brooms; you really should try and convince Sara to give you another lesson."

"It's not Sara who needs convincing," I replied. After all, my last experience on a broom had not ended that well.

"Well, you know what they say. When you fall off the broom, you just have to get right back up and try again."

"Yeah, I know the saying. Still, it's a lot easier to say

than to do. Now that a few days have gone past, it feels harder, mentally."

"Of course it will, but you really have no other choice. I don't like the broom myself; I don't like being high up in the air, and I generally just hover a few feet off the ground. However, it comes with being a witch, and you can't truly be a part of the coven if you don't know how to ride. Besides, it gives you a lot more freedom. Like being able to get from the diner to home in two minutes instead of ten."

As the smell of the delicious burgers wafted up to me through the bag, I couldn't help but think that was the best argument I had ever heard for learning to ride.

~

"You ou guys are lifesavers," Sara exclaimed as soon as we walked through the door. Since Chestnut was running around my ankles at top speed, I figured Ellie had come home from work.

"Can you take these?" Amy asked. "I have to go give Kevin his medicine before we eat." Kevin was Amy's familiar, a grey owl who suited her perfectly. Unfortunately, he had come down with the same ailment that had afflicted all of the owls in town for the past week, which was basically some sort of infection that stopped them from flying. The healers had come up with a potion to help, but it was still going to be a couple of days before Kevin was back to his normal self, and he was hiding away in Amy's room until he was back to normal.

"Of course," Sara said, taking the large bag full of curly fries from Amy's hands as she ran up the stairs to go take care of her familiar.

I followed after Sara into the kitchen along with the burgers I was carrying, where we found Ellie already getting plates and cutlery out.

"I was hoping you would stop at Two Wizards," Ellie said with a smile. "It's my favorite, even though my waistline always yells at me when I eat there."

"So the food is good?"

"It has to be here," Ellie replied. "After all, the population is so small that anybody who opens a less-than-stellar restaurant quickly goes out of business. But yes, Two Wizards is definitely one of the best places to eat. The food is good, and they have a really cool vibe there."

"I noticed that; it seems to be one of the few places in town where everything seems to be just like in the human world, instead of having magic infused into everything."

Ellie nodded. "Exactly. I think that's what made it popular at first; it's a little bit of a novelty to have something so exotic as a pure human restaurant here."

I bit back a smile; evidently what Ellie considered exotic, I considered completely normal, and I was happy to have a restaurant like that around for exactly the opposite reason as Ellie was.

Five minutes later we were all seated on the various couches and lounge chairs in the living room. All eyes turned to Sara, just as she took a huge bite into her burger, and we had to wait about forty-five seconds before she finished chewing and swallowing.

"Some witches can't do that elegantly," Ellie teased, and Sara stuck her tongue out at her.

"How was I supposed to know you were going to pick that exact second to ask me questions?"

"Well, you probably could have guessed, given as none of us had an acquaintance die on us this morning."

Sara scowled. "Yeah, I could do without repeating that."

"At least you haven't been arrested," I offered. "I mean, I'm sure Chief Enforcer King knows that you didn't do it, but I could have understood if she wanted to question you or whatever."

Sara nodded. "Yes, I'm pretty sure I'm in the clear. Of course, there are no guarantees, and Chief Enforcer King did ask me not to leave town, but I do have my freedom for now. My job, I don't know about. I don't even know what to do. Do I show up tomorrow like normal? Will someone just escort me off the premises if I'm not welcome? Is it going to be the most embarrassing moment of my life?"

"It's a law office, Sara, the last thing they want is

negative publicity," Amy said. "The people there are intelligent; if they're going to fire you, they're either going to tell you ahead of time, or when you show up to work tomorrow somebody will kindly and gently get you to leave without making a scene."

What Amy said definitely made sense, and I found myself nodding along in agreement. Sara evidently felt the same way; she looked a little bit less terrified than she had a moment earlier.

"Anyway, you haven't given us any of the juicy details yet. Did you find out anything about the murder?" Ellie asked, leaning forward in her chair as she munched on a curly fry.

Sara shrugged. "I did my best, but the enforcers weren't very into talking to me. It turns out when you're a murder suspect the police don't want to tell you everything they know about the victim."

"You had to have at least overheard something though, right?" I asked.

Sara nodded. "I did, yeah. But not a lot. I do know that Lorondir was poisoned. That actually works well in my favor; in all likelihood he would've ingested the poison before getting on my broom, which makes me less likely to be the killer."

Amy nodded. "We had suspected that was the case. It made the most sense, but it's good to have it confirmed. I suppose you didn't overhear what type of poison was used? I imagine they wouldn't even know yet."

"That's right," Sara said. "Chief Enforcer King used a potion to detect the poison in the first place, and she said it was going to take some more testing with the body before she would know exactly what type."

"Well, in our travels, we managed to happen across a pretty good suspect," I said, relaying to Sara and Ellie what Amy and I had discovered about Jordan Black.

"Wow, he's here?" Ellie said, her eyes widening. "I remember reading all about that case. It was a brutal murder, and everyone thought he was guilty. I don't think it came as a surprise to anyone when Black was found guilty, and we all thought he was going to go to jail for the rest of his life. Then he fired Lorondir, and his new lawyer got him off on a technicality."

"Do you know what that technicality was?" Amy asked, looking over at Ellie.

"No, I don't have a clue. The sites that I read my gossip on aren't exactly the most in-depth when it comes to specifics of the law. Plus, I think a lot of that information was kept a little bit hush-hush. Probably because the entire magical world thought Black was guilty."

"And if he was, he might have just committed a second murder," I said in a quiet voice. Sara, on the other couch, shivered.

"Is there any other opportunity for me to get involved, perhaps you need a martial arts expert to join you in the future?" Mr. Meowgi asked, making an appearance. He took the opportunity to try and nab a curly fry off my plate, but I was too quick for him and he scowled at me like I'd just kicked his best friend.

"I don't want you getting involved this time, please. After all, I wouldn't be able to stand it if you got hurt again."

"Please. Did Bruce Lee ever get hurt while participating in martial arts?"

"Um, I'm pretty sure he hurt his back pretty badly doing weights one time."

"Well, I don't do any weight training, mainly because they haven't invented dumbbells for those of us without opposable thumbs. I'm all about agility, baby."

I bit back a smile and gave my familiar a pat on the head. "All right, well, I'll keep you in mind for the future."

"That's all I ask," Mr. Meowgi replied, darting out a paw and grabbing at a curly fry sitting on the edge of my plate, running out of the room with his newfound prey in his mouth. "See? Agility!"

The others giggled as I scowled at my familiar.

"What *is* our next move, anyway?" I asked.

"Now we have to hunt down and interview someone who almost certainly committed one murder, if not two," Ellie said.

Great. This didn't sound dangerous at all.

CHAPTER 7

"I don't understand why I can't just learn this stuff from a book," I complained to Ellie a couple of hours later as we made our way through the large forest that made up the boundary of Western Woods. It was after seven now, and while there were still almost ninety minutes until sunset, the sun was definitely starting to drop in the sky, and going deep into the forest wasn't going to help.

Ellie shot me a look. "It's all good and fine to learn what the different plants look like from a book, but when the day comes that you have to find your own thornweed in the forest, it's definitely going to look different than the example on your page. Potions, and the herbology that goes with it, our lessons learned from the earth. You have to go to the earth to learn them properly."

This was my second lesson with Ellie; after we had

finished eating I grabbed my notebook that I had chosen to use for potions - I had bought a number of *Harry Potter*-themed journals on my trip back to the human world before moving here permanently - and pulled out a pen.

"I prefer spells to this; when you're learning spells you're not also fighting off mosquitoes."

"You could always do both," Ellie said with a wink. *"Jupiter, god of thunder, drive away the bloodsucker."*

"Okay, that's pretty cool," I said as a mosquito buzzed nearby but didn't land on me.

"See? The more you study, the more useful spells you learn. Now, come over here and let me show you the main herbs and plants you need to know about. Do you know what the basic cooking herbs look like?"

"I did a Buzzfeed quiz once, and I got, like, six out of twelve on it, so sort of?"

"I don't know what Buzzfeed is, but I think we can work with that," Ellie said. "Do you know what herb this is?" she asked, leaning down into the brush and coming back up with the leaf that I'd seen far too many times on Italian pasta sauce labels.

"Basil," I said confidently with a nod.

"Good."

"Can you find things like this anywhere?" I asked. "Or are there special parts of the forest where you have to go to find certain herbs?"

"For the most part, the most common herbs grow in most parts of the forest. Over the years, the witches and wizards of Western Woods planted multiple samples of everything all over so that it wouldn't be difficult for witches and wizards making potions to find the ingredients they needed. However, if you do know where to look, some parts of the forest have more of one herb than another. That's way more advanced than what you need to know right now, though."

I watched as Ellie picked up some of the basil and placed it inside a small leather pouch that she had brought with her.

"You're taking the basil home?"

"Yes," Ellie nodded. "It's important that you be able to recognize the fresh herbs, since some recipes call for herbs that are fresh - picked within an hour of being inserted into the potion - but some require herbs that have been dried. So, since we are out here anyway, I figured I might as well grab a few herbs to increase my dried collection."

I nodded and helped Ellie by finding some more basil as well.

"Do you recognize this one?" Ellie asked a few minutes later, holding up a different leaf. This one was definitely different; the leaves were very long, and shaped like rather thin ovals. The veins are quite visible, and it had almost a fuzzy look to it.

I furrowed my brow in concentration; I knew I had seen it somewhere before, but I couldn't quite place it.

"It's sage," Ellie said when I shook my head. "Here,

take it. Learn how it feels in your hands, and learn how it looks."

Taking out my notebook, I drew a picture of the leaf as I ran it between my fingers.

"What is sage generally used for?"

"While there are no strict rules - I've seen sage used in potions for everything from healing salves to potions meant to make someone act crazy - in general sage is used for a lot of healing potions. That's where you'll find it most often as an ingredient."

I nodded as I wrote down what Ellie said, and when she had picked up enough of the sage, we moved on.

"Is it hard to make, the potion that makes people act crazy? I feel like that would be a fun one to play pranks with," I said with a grin to Ellie as we continued to walk through the forest.

"It's pretty tough, yeah. Plus, it's one of the regulated potions. If you don't have a license to make it, you're not allowed to do so."

"Really? That exists?"

"Of course. After all, potions can be used for all sorts of unethical reasons, and so over the centuries witches and wizards determined that they had to be controlled. For example, what would you do if you had a potion that would increase your short-term memory significantly?"

I thought about it for a second. "Well, it would have made high school a lot easier."

"Exactly. We can't have witches and wizards at the

Academy going around taking potions to increase their intelligence level artificially. So, those sorts of potions are all regulated as well. Although, as with anything else that's illegal, there are always ways to get around it."

"Did you ever take some of the memory enhancing potion?" I asked with a grin, and Ellie gave me a sly smile.

"I'll never admit this in front of Amy, since even though it was ten years ago she'd probably still turn me in for doing it. But yes, a friend of mine had an older brother who wasn't exactly on the right side of the law a lot of the time, and he managed to procure some for us that originated in a Polynesian paranormal community. He smuggled it back into Western Woods, and sold it to my friend's brother, who then sold it to us."

"Did it work?"

"Let's put it this way: it was the first and last time in my life I've ever had a better score than Amy on a test."

My eyes widened. "Okay, so it does work. That's pretty cool."

Before I had a chance to ask anything else about the restricted use potions, a rustling sound came from deeper in the forest. I froze, all too aware that this place was full of shifters, and I didn't want to find myself face to face with a lion, or a grizzly bear, or whatever.

"What was that?" I asked, gripping Ellie by the arm.

"Probably a deer," Ellie said, completely relaxed.

"Don't worry, the shifters aren't allowed to shift until after nightfall, and there's no reason for anyone to have hired a shifter to scare you right now."

Great. That made me feel *way* better.

When, a minute later, I heard the same sound again, only this time much closer, I began to panic for real.

"Well now, what are two witches doing in the forest?" a voice asked from nearby, and I nearly jumped out of my skin. Still, I recognized the voice. It was Kyran, an elf I'd met a couple of times already here in Western Woods, who didn't seem to have a great reputation with everybody else, but who I thought seemed friendly enough.

He popped out from behind a tree, and I inhaled sharply as I caught sight of him. Dark hair that was just long enough to give him a permanent just-got-out-of-bed look framed his pointed elf ears, and his eyes were so blue it was like looking into a glacial lake. Even though he was dressed casually, wearing khakis and a polo shirt instead of the long robes elves usually wore, the muscular tone of his body still stood out.

"You're Kyran, aren't you?" Ellie asked, her eyes narrowing in suspicion.

"Sure am," Kyran said with a grin.

"We don't want any trouble, just get out of here," Ellie said.

"Hey, I don't want any trouble either," Kyran replied, opening his hands. "I just don't usually find witches in the forest here, that's all."

"Ellie's teaching me all about the herbs," I said. "So I can make potions."

"Good," Kyran said, nodding. "Potions wouldn't be affected by the fact that you don't know who your true coven is. You'll be much better at potions than spells until you discover your people."

I shot him a grin. "You sound a bit like a wizard yourself."

"Don't say that in front of everybody else, you'll get kicked out of the coven," Kyran told me with a wink. Ellie looked at me like I'd just spouted an extra head. Evidently, she had not been looking forward to a conversation with Kyran.

"Come on, Tina. Let's get out of here," Ellie said, grabbing me by the arm and practically dragging me back towards town.

"See you around," Kyran said, evidently not bothered in the least by the fact that Ellie had practically run away from him. I shot him a wave and a smile as I was dragged away, and as soon as we reached the road once more, Ellie turned on me.

"Do you know who that guy was?" she practically hissed. "He's so dangerous."

"Who, Kyran? He seems nice. Everyone seems to hate him, but no one really tells me why."

"Kyran grew up in Western Woods," Ellie started. "Mind you, this was before my time. He's quite young by Elven standards. I think he's like four hundred years old or something. He's basically the elf equivalent of our age. His family is one of the original Elven families. We don't even know where they come from. His father is thousands of years old. Anyway, instead of going into one of the intelligence positions like all the other elves, like becoming a lawyer or an accountant, Kyran had decided he wanted to work security and law enforcement instead."

"And let me guess, it was decided that he couldn't do it?" I said with a wry smile. Western Woods had very specific ideas as to which paranormals could perform which jobs.

"Of course not," Ellie said. "He was an elf. He was supposed to go into a job that elves perform. Anyway, eventually Kyran actually went and tried to apply for a job as an enforcer, and he was basically laughed out of the place. His reputation was ruined, and he decided that if he wasn't going to get a job as an enforcer, he was going to make his own job."

"So? Lots of people work for themselves."

"Yeah, but lots of other people don't hunt other paranormals."

My mouth dropped open. "What?"

"Kyran decided that he was going to fill a hole in the law enforcement community. Basically, well we have enforcers to make sure that the laws in the paranormal world are enforced, when it comes to law enforcement in the human world, things get a lot trickier. For one thing, jurisdiction becomes an issue. If Western Woods was to send out an enforcer to make sure paranormals weren't taking advantage of humans, who was to say where that spot would end? After all, there is a vampire-exclusive community just north of here, called Vampouver. What if our enforcer went into territory that they considered theirs? There would be diplomatic issues involved. So, as a result, most paranormal communities choose to simply ignore the human world."

"Wait, does that mean that there are paranormals that come in to the human world and like, attack people?"

"It doesn't happen often, but it does happen. You would read them as events where something absolutely extraordinary seemed to happen, and you call them freak accidents. They're often not freak accidents at all, but rather the work of paranormals."

"So what does Kyran have to do with this? Does he go into the human world and hurt people?" I had trouble believing that the friendly elf that I knew would do something so horrible.

"No, he goes into the human world and he stops the paranormals himself."

"So he's basically elf Batman?"

"What's a Batman?"

"Never mind. But so, he's a vigilante that makes sure paranormals who go to the human world to commit crime are punished?"

Ellie nodded. "That's right," she said. "Generally, once he catches someone, he brings them back here and they're prosecuted. After all, there are laws against committing acts of mischief in the human world. They're just not enforced, normally."

"Wait, so why is everyone so scared of him? I mean, he's a good guy, right?"

"But he does this on his own," Ellie said. "He's an elf. He's not supposed to be going around doing the work that essentially belongs to shifters."

"So what if he does?" I asked. "If he likes what he does, and ultimately he does good work, isn't that better than having him sitting behind a desk doing work he absolutely hates all day?"

Ellie's brow furrowed. "I mean, when you put it that way, I guess so. But the point is, it's not natural."

I struggled not to laugh. I couldn't believe that the reason everyone seemed to be avoiding Kyran was because he didn't take the same sort of job that he was supposed to.

"Who made up these rules about who has to take what job, anyway?" I asked. "It seems rather arcane and arbitrary."

"It's just how it's always been," Ellie said with a shrug. "Paranormal communities have worked this way for thousands of years.

"That doesn't mean things have to stay that way."

"Well, you're still new here, you'll get used to how we do things eventually," Ellie said confidently.

"Maybe," I said, unconvinced. "But I don't think you'll ever get me to believe that all paranormals of one species should all fit into the same mold, and I think you should all cut Kyran a little bit of slack, especially since he's doing good things."

"You just like him because he looks good without a shirt on," Ellie said to me with a wink. I tried to stop the blush from crawling up my face, but failed miserably. Ellie laughed as we reached the house, evidently pleased with herself for managing to embarrass me.

I couldn't believe that was the only thing everyone had against Kyran; that he went against the paranormal world's norms when it came to a person's role in society. I shook my head and followed after her into the house.

CHAPTER 8

*T*he next morning, Amy decided we were going to visit Lita at the coven headquarters. After all, a couple of days earlier we had discovered that I was, in all likelihood, originally from a coven whose celestial influence was a water planet or moon.

"We need to tell her," Amy said. "It might influence how I should be teaching you spells, after all."

Lita Sahera, the head of the coven of Jupiter, worked out of coven headquarters, a whitewashed brick building the size of a large house with a green dome on top.

The last time I had been here, Chief Enforcer King had knocked on the door and it was Amy herself who had answered. She worked for Lita at times, when she wasn't doing her advanced studies at the coven Academy. This time, however, Amy simply opened the door herself and let us in.

Another young witch scrambled over to the door, but when she saw it was Amy, she stopped.

"Oh, it's just you," she said.

"Yes, I'm bringing Tina here over to see Lita," Amy replied loftily.

"Well, I'm not sure the head of the coven has the time to see you at the moment," the other girl said haughtily.

"Seeing as Tina is in my care, and I was specifically told by Lita to take charge of her education, I think Lita will make time to see me," Amy said. Wow. There was obviously no love lost between these two. I looked from one to the other, as the two of them shot daggers at each other. Well, maybe lightning bolts was more appropriate, given as they both belonged to the coven of thunder.

"Come on Tina," Amy ordered, making her way down the hall. The other woman scrambled after us, making her way into Lita's office about a second before us.

"I'm so sorry, she just burst in here," the girl said, and Lita stood up from the lounge chair she was reading at, smiling as soon as she noticed Amy and me.

"Not to worry, Estelle. Amy and Tina are completely welcome. Please, come in."

Amy shot Estelle a triumphant look as the two of us slipped past her and into the room. I gave Estelle a friendly smile – after all, it sounded like she was just following protocol – but got a glare in return. Apparently, Estelle wasn't a huge fan of mine already.

She strode past us and out of the room as Lita motioned for Amy and me to have a seat. Lita was absolutely the picture-perfect image of the bustling, friendly Italian mom. I half expected her to bring out a plate of lasagna and encourage us to eat up, complaining that we were too thin.

"It's lovely to see the both of you," Lita said, her dark curls bobbing up and down as she moved over to her desk. "To what can I attribute this wonderful visit?"

"We think we may have an indication as to Tina's coven of origin, and I thought we should let you know," Amy said, her hands crossed in front of her. Totally a Hermione move.

Lita's face lit up. "Really? Wonderful. Please, tell me everything."

Amy turned to me, and I recalled the entire experience, when I had seen Mr. Meowgi injured, and a spell I didn't recognize burst out of me. I had been standing in a water fountain at the time, and the spell I'd used had shot water at the attacker, cursed water that had apparently maimed his face permanently.

As the story continued, Lita looked more and more serious, and when I finally finished, she exhaled loudly, leaning back in her chair.

"Wow. I knew a powerful spell had been cast, since Chief Enforcer King told me about it, but I didn't know that it was *you* who had performed it, Tina. I believe, from what you've told me, that Amy's suspicions are true, as they usually are. You're almost certainly a witch from a coven guided by water. Now we simply need to discover which one. I've already put some feelers out to the heads of other covens out there as we try to determine your origins, and being able to narrow it down to a single element will certainly help."

"Amy told me there were tons of water-guided covens," I said.

"Well, yes, that is true. But it still narrows our search down from thousands of covens to the low hundreds."

My heart sunk at the raw numbers. "So there's still basically no chance of finding my coven based on this."

Lita shook her head. "It's unlikely, but it's a start, and it's much more information than we had before. Amy, if you don't mind, I would like you to test out Tina's powers in the water, if possible. Do you have access to a large amount of water near your home?"

Even Amy and her stoic look couldn't hide the grin that popped up. After all, I had totally planned on lounging in the new addition to our backyard that afternoon after magic lessons with Amy.

"We most certainly do," Amy replied. "That won't be a problem."

"Good. Thank you for taking this on, Amy."

"It's not a problem, I'm just glad Tina isn't a total idiot."

I stifled a giggle as Lita gave Amy a stern look. "Even witches who aren't as talented as yourself deserve an education."

"I know, but I find it so much more difficult to teach the ones who don't understand," Amy complained. "Luckily, Tina isn't that sort of witch at all. I taught her the illuminating spell, and her second attempt would have been almost passable at the academy, which is quite a feat for a spell from a different coven."

"That is impressive," Lita said, her eyebrows rising as she turned towards me. A blush crawled up my face; I wasn't used to being spoken about as though I was particularly skilled at anything. I had never been *bad* in school or anything like that, but I certainly wasn't good, either. A B average was my mainstay, and much like everything else in life, I was completely average. I liked it that way. This praise made me feel kind of uncomfortable.

"I think so, too," Amy agreed with a nod. "I will continue her training. Let us know if you need anything else from us."

"Well, one thing I would like to know, Tina, while I have you here, is how you're finding everything. Are people being friendly to you? Are you being welcomed into town? How are you finding magic?"

The caring look on Lita's face told me she actually cared about the answers.

"It's been really nice, for the most part. Amy, Sara,

and Ellie are all amazing, and I'm not just saying that because Amy is sitting next to me. It's been really nice of all of them to teach me their particular skills, and I really do appreciate that they've accepted me into their home."

"That's excellent to hear and I would have expected no less. What about the others in town?"

"Um, that's been a little bit more complex," I admitted. "After all, a decent number of the citizens here thought I was a murderer until a couple of days ago. That said, there have been more friendly faces than not."

"Good, I'm happy to hear it. Jackson Lupo came to see me about the incident with his shifter who got a little bit overly enthusiastic while you were on the broom."

I hated to admit it, but my heart skipped a beat at the thought of the leader of the shifter pack. With his long, blonde hair and casual confidence, I liked Jackson as soon as I'd met him. Still, I was a grown woman, and I shouldn't be acting like this just at the mention of him.

"Yes, Jormund came to see me and apologized in person," I nodded. "I accepted his apology."

"I'm glad to hear he came to see you in person," Lita said. "I had some strong words with Jackson, and he promised me that sort of thing will not happen again."

Amy coughed slightly, and Lita turned to her.

"Tina is also friends with Kyrandir, I believe," Amy

said, and I shot a glare her way. Way to tattle on your friends. Then again, there was no reason why I *shouldn't* interact with Kyran, especially after what Ellie had told me. The only reason he was an outcast was because of what he chose to do for a living, and that was no reason to hate someone.

Lita pressed her lips together. "I won't tell Tina not to interact with someone she finds friendly in town," she said, replying to me. "However, I would caution you against spending too much time with that elf, simply because with you already being new, you don't want to be alienated as well."

My heart sank. Even Lita was telling me not to spend time with Kyran, as it would ruin my own reputation here in town.

"Now, have you given any thought as to what you would like to do as a job, when your magic skills are up to scratch?" Lita asked, quickly changing subjects.

I shook my head. "Not really. I think maybe something in healing would suit me. I was thinking of going into nursing when I was in the human world. I also considered maybe doing something with animal healing, but that doesn't seem to be a thing here."

"No, the regular Healers take care of that, when it's needed," Lita said.

"But Heather – Sara's mom – didn't seem to know much about animals when she had to take care of Mr. Meowgi."

"No, they're not trained in it."

"Would that be a possible option? Leaning to treat only animals, and healing them?"

Lita thought carefully. "I'm not certain. It sounds like it could be a good idea, if you managed to get the training for it."

I smiled. Even though it wasn't definitely a green light, I was pretty sure I had just figured out what I was going to do as a job here in Western Woods. I was going to be the first ever magical vet.

CHAPTER 9

As we left the coven headquarters, Estelle scowled at us on the way out.

"What does she have against you?" I asked. "I was half expecting her to try and stab you."

"Estelle is the daughter of Ariadne, the woman who almost wouldn't sell you a wand the other day," Amy explained. "She's extremely ambitious, and thinks she's the smartest witch in the coven. She's not, of course, but that doesn't stop her from trying to one-up me at any opportunity."

I hid a smile. So this was what happened when two goodie-two-shoes tried to one-up each other at every opportunity.

"Did you mean it, what you said about learning to be a healer for animals?" Amy asked.

I nodded. "I hadn't really thought about it too much

before, but yeah, if that's an avenue that's open, I think I would like to do it."

"Despite the fact that it's new, and that no one does it right now, I think that's actually a very good idea. After all, when all the owls in town got sick, there was no one to go to specifically. It took a couple of days before the Healers were able to come up with a potion to make them better. For a while, we didn't even know if it would be possible. I think having a healer dedicated to animals is important, especially given how many witches there are around here with familiars. I would love it if there was someone who could specifically care for Kevin."

I was touched; I honestly didn't expect Amy to be on my side. After all, this place seemed to be pretty strict when it came to what jobs were available for witches.

"It's probably a ways away yet, still. After all, I know how to do one spell, and even though I've learned the happiness potion, I'm only just learning the names of most of the herbs that we use here, and I really know nothing about healing anybody, let alone animals."

"Sure, but I think having a goal will help you. After all, now you're not just learning magic for the sake of it. You're learning magic to help you heal animals in the future."

I smiled at Amy as we made our way back home.

"I'm going to head off; I wanted to stop by the library and check on a few things before coming back home, and then I'm working at headquarters this afternoon," Amy said. "Do you think you can find your way back?"

"Of course," I nodded. "Not a problem."

Amy waved and headed off, and just as she did I realized we were only about a block away from Hexpresso Bean, and that Ellie's shift would be ending in about an hour. That would give me just enough time to enjoy a coffee, and maybe another delectable pastry, before I could join her in picking up Chestnut from doggie daycare and heading home.

The fairy manning the counter today was named Aurora; I had met her my first visit here and she had always been very friendly.

"Tina, how nice to see you," Aurora said with a smile, her golden wings fluttering behind her with excitement. "How are you settling into town? I hear we have you to thank for the fact that a murderer has been taken off our streets."

I flashed Aurora a smile. "Well, I wouldn't go that far. I definitely messed it up pretty badly, but luckily Sara and Amy got me out of hot water."

"Well, either way, whatever you want today is on the house. It's good to be able to walk home at night again without worrying about being attacked."

"Thank you so much," I said, warmth rising in my heart. It was so nice of Aurora to do this for me. "Can I get a coffee and one of Ellie's amazing cinnamon buns?" I asked.

"Of course! And let me tell you, the cinnamon buns today are absolutely amazing. She's outdone herself," Aurora added with a wink.

"That's great to hear," I laughed. "Hey, could you tell Ellie that I'm here, and that I'll wait until her shift is over for her to come out?"

"You've got it," Aurora said. "Grab a seat anywhere, and I'll bring it out. You know the drill by now."

Thanking Aurora once again, I found a free spot in a tiny, two-person booth at the back of the café. It was private, and kept me hidden away from the rest of the patrons of the coffee shop, which was just how I liked it. I didn't like being the center of attention here, which was kind of natural when I was the only new paranormal this town had seen in goodness knew how long.

A couple of minutes later, Aurora came back with my coffee and cinnamon bun, and I found a copy of the local newspaper, The Magic Word, at a spare table nearby. Flipping through the articles, I ate my cinnamon bun but quickly found my mind wandering instead to the murder of Lorondir.

Jordan Black seemed like an obvious suspect, but how on earth were we going to find him? After all, it was possible he had already left town, anyway. I mean, if I was going to commit a murder of my former lawyer in his town on the other side of the world from where I lived, I would definitely skip town as soon as possible.

I wondered if Kyran would know how to find him.

After all, if he was the type to hunt down criminals in the human world, maybe he would know a little bit about hunting down criminals in the paranormal world as well.

That was when I realized I didn't even know how to get in touch with Kyran if I wanted to. He just kind of showed up sometimes.

The cinnamon bun was definitely one of Ellie's best, and as I devoured it, I let my mind wander just a little bit more.

"I can't believe someone killed him," I suddenly heard a voice behind me say, and I was jolted back to reality. The voice was female, and low, very Demi Moore-like.

"Can't you?" a male voice replied. "I told you not get involved with him. He was bad news."

"He was one of the best criminal lawyers in the world, and that was what I needed. I mean, I'm looking at serious time here. I needed somebody who could get me off the hook."

"Just like he got that shifter off the hook? No, the old elf was losing it. No wonder he was retiring."

My eyes widened as I realized the conversation behind me concerned Lorondir. Obviously, whoever was at the table behind me didn't realize there was anyone in this booth.

"Well, he might have been retiring, but he was going to see my case through to the end. And it wasn't because of anything *he* did that he was retiring, he was taking care of that loser son of his."

"Farawir?"

"That's right."

"What about him?"

A cold, hard laugh escaped the woman's lips. "You don't have your ear to the underground as well as you used to, Victor. Farawir's gotten himself into a spot of trouble, and daddy has had to come over and rescue him from it."

"Gambling? Again? I thought he kicked that habit a hundred years back."

"Yeah, well, you know how it is. A hundred years without gambling, then suddenly you see a sure thing, you make one bet, and it's all downhill from there."

"So the old man is retiring to hang onto his reputation?"

"And apparently set up his son for a while," the woman answered. "That's what I've heard, anyway."

"Well, regardless, you're going to have to find a new lawyer, now."

The woman sighed.

"I'm aware. I don't know who else to go to. Lorondir was the best there was."

"He really wasn't. He was pretty good, but he wasn't the best. You don't need to look just at the local lawyers, anyway. There are lots of good ones elsewhere."

"Still, I liked the lawyer I had. Anyway, I've got to

go. I definitely need a stiff drink after getting this news."

The chair behind me scraped just as Ellie sat down in front of me.

"Do you know who it is who just got up from that chair?" I whispered to her in a hushed voice. Ellie had a quick look.

"Sure. Maria, one of the local vampires."

"We have to follow her."

"Ok."

I loved how Ellie didn't even question why. She just accepted that we had to do it. Giving the vampire about a fifteen second head start, Ellie and I got up and passed by her companion, who with his silver hair, deep brown eyes and sharp fangs was also definitely a vampire.

When we got back onto the street, my shoulders slumped as I realized I couldn't see the vampire at all.

"Where'd she go?" I asked.

Ellie squinted in the sun. "It's probably too bright for her to spend much time out here. She may have changed into a bat to go wherever her next stop was. Do you have any idea what that was?"

"She said she needed to get a drink."

Ellie grinned. "Good. Then we're going to The Bloody Mary."

Yeah, that didn't sound ominous at all.

CHAPTER 10

"The Bloody Mary is the local vampire bar," Ellie explained as she led me down the street.

"Wow, you all really don't like to hang out with different species, do you?"

"Well, for vampires it's really different. For one thing, their bar doesn't actually open until the sun rises, usually around six or seven in the morning. So for us, obviously, that doesn't really work. They'll keep drinking until the middle of the afternoon, at which point the vampire's last call is at 2pm, and then they head home to sleep it off."

I laughed. I hadn't actually considered that vampires would really keep opposite hours to the rest of the paranormals. "Ok, that's definitely a good reason to have a different bar," I said.

"Vampires can be a little bit threatening when you

first meet them," Ellie explained. "Don't let the leering put you off, that's just how they are."

"Ok."

Ellie stopped in front of a small, wooden house, and took the steps that led down towards a door at basement level. On the black door was painted a single white fang, with drops of blood dripping from it. The painting had obviously been done quite a while back, as it was faded in quite a few spots, but it was enough for me to know we were in the right place. This was definitely The Bloody Mary.

As soon as Ellie opened the door a hiss emanated from the crowd inside. I slipped in behind her and closed the door quickly, letting my eyes adjust to the darkness. Because yeah, it was *really* dark in here. A couple of candles hanging from chandeliers on the ceiling gave off small bursts of light here and there, but that was it. I could just make out a large bar over to the right. It was smooth and sleek, and pure black, as was the shelf behind it. The tables and chairs were all modern in style; it was all quite different to The Magic Mule, which was the bar for witches and wizards in town.

Sitting at a table in the back corner was the vampire I'd seen at the coffee shop. I could make out long, dark curly hair that framed a pale face, eagerly sipping at the drink she'd just been brought by another vampire. It was red, obviously. A bloody Mary, I assumed. I hoped.

The vampire at the bar looked us over for a minute,

then motioned for us to make our way to him. He was young-looking, with a thin mustache and dark hair that crossed over his almost-black eyes, half hiding them from view.

"What brings two witches into this fine establishment today?" he asked with a grin, showing off his fangs. I didn't like the way he looked Ellie and I up and down, like he was absolutely judging us and didn't care that we had noticed.

"We're looking for one of your patrons."

"Oh? And what might you be after?"

"Information," I said. "About Lorondir."

"Ah, the dead elf. Well then, off you go. I'm not allowed to serve witches and wizards alcohol; my license doesn't permit it, so you'll excuse me if I don't offer you a drink."

"Right, like we'd want one from you anyway," Ellie muttered, earning herself a glare from the bartender. I liked her spunk. She grabbed me by the arm and led me away from the bartender, who winked at me as I was dragged off. Ugh. I was going to have to take a shower after I left here; I already felt disgusting.

Ellie and I made our way towards the vampire, and as we got closer to her table, she looked up at us. Her eyes showed a little bit of confusion, but her expression didn't change.

"What do you want?" she asked.

Ellie took the initiative and sat down at the table in front of her. "We want to help you."

"Oh yeah? How's that?" A single dark eyebrow rose on the vampire's face. She bared her teeth slightly, allowing her fangs to show just a little bit. I had a feeling that vampires used that move to be a little bit threatening.

"Your lawyer. He was killed yesterday."

"Yeah, so he was. So?"

"So, our friend got caught up in the investigation, and we're trying to figure out who killed the elf to get her name out of it," I explained.

"What's that got to do with me?"

"Chief Enforcer King would probably be pretty happy to hear if information you gave us helped find the killer," Ellie said, crossing her arms. "After all, biting people is a pretty serious offense, and you're looking at some pretty heavy jail time."

My eyes widened as I realized who we were talking to. This was Maria Grecu, the vampire who had bitten another vampire. I felt a bit silly for not having made that connection earlier. Great. What if she bit us? Could witches turn into vampires? I had no idea how any of this worked. Ellie didn't seem scared at all, but Ellie really didn't seem scared about anything. And besides, she had a whole host of spells in her repertoire that she could use to defend herself; I definitely didn't.

Maria looked at each of us in turn, then finally bared her fangs once more before sighing deeply and leaning back. She motioned with her hands for us to keep talking. "All right, what you want to know?"

"What do you know about Lorondir's son and his gambling addiction?" I asked.

Maria grinned, but it wasn't a nice smile. "That elf is a piece of work. Not only does he have a gambling addiction, but he's been arrested in at least three different paranormal towns for violence, he's been banned from five others, and he's tried to outrun his debts a couple of times over the years. Things came to a head right around the turn of the last century, when Lorondir ended up having to pay millions of abras to some very bad people to get them off his son's back. After that, he hired someone to take care of his son, and the kid eventually kicked the addiction. He took it up again about a month back, but I don't think Lorondir knew about his son's relapse."

'Abras', I had learned, referred to the local currency, Abracadollars.

"So his dad didn't even know?" I asked.

Maria shook her head and smiled again. "No, and the most hilarious part is, when I was in his office last week, I overheard him talking to that other elf that works there, the female one. He was changing his will. I suspect he was actually including his son in it for the first time in years."

Ellie and I glanced at each other. Now all of a sudden we had a son who not only probably had a grudge against his dad, definitely had a gambling addiction and a history of violence, and was possibly going to come into some money if his dad turned up dead?

It looked like Jordan Black wasn't the only person in Western Woods with a pretty good motive for committing murder.

"That other elf, was her name Manarwa?" I asked.

"That's the one," Maria nodded.

I bit my lip as I considered our options. There was no way Manarwa was going to tell us about the will; I had seen enough crime TV to know about attorney-client privilege, and I figured it also applied here, too. After all, if she had been at liberty to say anything, Manarwa might have done so when Amy and I went to speak with her.

"Who do you think killed your lawyer?" Ellie asked.

Maria shrugged. "Wouldn't have a clue. I put my money on that kid though. I know a few people have said Jordan Black is back in town, and goodness knows he probably wants the elf dead, but Farawir has had it in for his father for hundreds of years. Trust me, that's a lot of time for a grudge to hold."

"How old are you?" I asked, the words coming out before I realize how it could have sounded. "Sorry, don't answer that if it was super rude."

Maria smiled at me. "You're that new witch, aren't you? I can tell. For one thing, the other one is smarter than you. She has her wand out underneath the table pointed at me just in case I try to bite either one of you.

Anyway, to answer your question, I was born seven hundred and twenty-two years ago."

My mouth gaped open at the answer. If I'd had to guess, I wouldn't have pegged her as a day over thirty-five.

Maria's smile turned into a grin of pleasure at my surprise. "I don't look a day over 500, do I? You've probably never really met many people my age, have you?"

I shook my head, not trusting my mouth to make words. This woman was over seven hundred years old? That was insane.

"Are vampires immortal as well?"

"In the same way as elves are, yes. We can be killed, but only by stabbing. Poisons don't work on us, because our blood immediately filters the poisons out. You really haven't spent any time in the paranormal world, have you?"

I shook my head. "No, sorry if my questions seem impertinent. I just genuinely don't know the answer to a lot of these things."

Maria grinned. "Well, better to find out than to live in ignorance. You'll do well here, especially if you hang out with your friends until you learn to stop being so naïve. Vampires aren't inherently scary, but there are bad apples in every species, and many people would consider me one of those bad apples."

"Are you one?"

"My lawyer probably wouldn't want me to answer that, even though he's dead."

"Do you know where to find Jordan Black?" Ellie asked, getting the conversation back on track.

Maria shook her head. "I don't even know for sure that he's even in town. It was just a rumor that I heard, but if you ask Adrian behind the bar, he might know."

"Thanks," I said as Ellie stood up. "Sorry about your lawyer."

Maria shrugged. "It happens. It's just too bad there's not another criminal lawyer in town anywhere near as good as Lorondir."

The two of us got up and headed back towards the bar.

"Was Lorondir that good?" I asked Ellie. "After all, the guy she was with at the coffee shop seemed to think he was overrated."

"If you'd asked me before the Jordan Black trial, I would have said for sure he was the best. But, ever since then, his reputation has definitely taken a bit of a hit. I still think he's the best criminal lawyer in town, and I don't think you'd find anyone who disagreed. But I can also see why he wanted to get out of the job now."

The two of us made our way back to the creepy bartender, and sat down on stools.

"I thought I told you two I couldn't serve you," he scowled at us.

"Were not here for alcohol, were here for information," Ellie said. "Maria said you could help us."

"Oh yeah? What is it you want to know?" He continued to wipe down the counter, seemingly uninterested in whatever we were talking about.

"Is Jordan Black in town?" Ellie asked, and the bartender stopped mid-wipe. He came over to us, speaking in hushed tones.

"Who told you that?"

"We're not at liberty to reveal our sources," I replied. "Is that a yes?"

The bartender nodded. "Yeah. He's here. Showed up a couple of nights ago. A friend of mine, who works the night shift at one of the local hotels, saw him come in. He asked for a room, for a room service menu, and not to be disturbed no matter what. He also paid my friend five hundred abras to keep quiet about what he saw."

"Wow, your friend sounds real trustworthy," Ellie said. The bartender glared at her.

"Hey, I'm helping you out here," he said. Ellie held up her hands in apology.

"Where is this? The place where he's staying?" I asked.

"Western Woods Lodge," the bartender replied. "I'm just telling you this so you'll get him in trouble. I don't like having people like him around town, and it wouldn't surprise me if he was the one who offed that lawyer elf."

I nodded. "So you think he killed that guy?"

"Of course he bloody did," the bartender replied, going back to wiping the counter, this time with more vigor. "Everyone knows it. Just because he got off on a technicality doesn't make him a good guy all of a sudden."

"Thanks," Ellie said with a nod. "We'll get out of here."

"Good, it makes the customers suspicious when we have non-vampires hanging around here for too long."

Moving to the end of the bar, the bartender didn't even look at us again as Ellie and I got up off our stools and made our way towards the exit. We slipped through the door as quickly as possible, a hiss of annoyance coming from the patrons once more, and as soon as we made our way back out into the bright sunshine of the day I blinked heavily, my eyes taking a while to get used to the bright sunshine.

"Well, that was illuminating," Ellie said.

"No kidding," I replied. "I think we need to get a look at that will Lorondir made just before he died."

"I was hoping you would say that."

CHAPTER 11

"*Y*ou know, when I said I was hoping we would get a look at it, I was kind of hoping to do it in a much more legal manner," I said as we sat in the kitchen, making a potion that would render us invisible for when we broke into the law offices where Lorondir worked later that night.

"You sound like Amy," Ellie said. "Besides, consider this a part of your education."

"Right, I'm sure making an invisibility potion in order to break into a local business is definitely what Lita was thinking of when she put you in charge of some of my teaching."

"Never mind, you're more whiny than Amy. Amy would just straight up refuse to do this."

I stuck my tongue out at Ellie, who motioned to a jar sitting on the counter.

"I need you to grab me that jar of birch bark," she said, and I did so. I mean, as much as I didn't want to break any laws or get in trouble, I also really wanted to know what was in Lorondir's new will, and if we were invisible there was no way we could get caught, right?

"Now, bark is especially important in a lot of potions, but you have to make sure that you have the bark from the right tree, and it has to be perfectly dry. Fresh bark is almost never an ingredient in any potions, and after you've removed the bark from a tree, it has to sit in the open air for at least three weeks before it's considered dry enough to use in potions. And it can't be rained on, either."

"So basically, you need to harvest all of the bark you possibly need for the year in the summer?" I asked.

"That's right," Ellie said. "At least, for amateur potions makers like us. There are professional outlets, and professional witches who deal in potions exclusively, and they tend to have their own private greenhouses set up, so that they can dry out the bark year-round. There's really no need for us to do that, though."

I nodded as I wrote down what Ellie had just told me in my journal.

"When this potion is finished, we need to freeze it for at least four hours."

"That'll give us time to go to Lorondir's funeral," Sara said from the doorway, where she was watching what was going on.

"Is that today?" I asked, and Sara nodded.

"When elves are killed, it's tradition that they need to have the ashes scattered within forty-eight hours of the death. Lorondir's family decided to do the release at sunset tonight."

"Good, we'll definitely go. That might give us an opportunity to have a look at that son Farawir and maybe get a handle on him."

"Hey, I meant to ask, do you guys have any pictures of Jordan Black? From like, old newspaper articles or anything? After all, I wouldn't put it past him to show up as well."

"Good thinking," Sara said, racing out of the room and returning a moment later with an old newspaper clipping. Staring back at me was the picture of a brooding, round-faced young man with deep set eyes and a hard mouth. He definitely looked like a bear, and as soon as I looked at it I knew that if I ran into him at the funeral, I would know it.

"You have to let me come to this, too," Mr. Meowgi said, making his way into the kitchen and sniffing at the potion before turning his nose up to it.

"I don't think pets are generally invited to funerals," I replied. "I mean, it was fine at the last one we went to, but only because that was for a wizard. Elves don't have familiars. At least, I don't think they do," I said, looking at Ellie and Sara expectantly.

"That's right," Ellie replied. "Only witches and wizards have familiars, and unfortunately for you, Mr.

Meowgi, I don't think you would be very welcome at an elf funeral."

"That's racist," my familiar muttered, sulking.

"Tell you what," I said, trying to cheer him up. "How about I promise that tomorrow, no matter what we do to investigate, you can come along with us?"

"I'm going to hold you to that," my cat said as he stalked out of the room. "Time to train to get ready."

A part of me didn't want to know what Mr. Meowgi considered martial arts training. As long as he didn't break anything, though, I supposed that was good enough.

"Is Amy going to be able to make it to the funeral? Sara asked, and Ellie shook her head.

"No, she's working all night. Although, I wouldn't be surprised if Lita goes and asks Amy to accompany her, in which case we might see her there."

Twenty minutes later, Ellie and I had finished making the potion - by which I meant Ellie made the potion, while I watched and took notes, as it was a significantly more complex potion than the one I had already made - and the three of us spent the afternoon relaxing before our long night ahead.

As the sun began to set, Sara, Ellie, and I got ready to go to the elf funeral.

"You want to wear all white," Ellie explained to me. "While witches and wizards follow the human tradition of wearing black to funerals, elves wear white exclusively."

"Thanks, good to know," I said as I put away the black blouse I was planning on wearing.

When we all left the house, I was wearing a simple sundress that I had bought at Randy Tonner's clothing store when I first arrived in Western Woods, whose color I could change by tapping it with my wand, making it now a pure white. Given as it was still mid-summer, and the heat wave in the Pacific Northwest seemed to show no sign of slowing down, it was definitely refreshing to be able to wear this outside.

I expected us to head downtown somewhere, but to my surprise, Ellie and Sara immediately turned off the road and onto the path that led to the forest.

"Where is this funeral taking place?" I asked.

"The elves have a sacred tree in the middle of the forest. It's completely white, and they scatter the ashes of all of their dead around it. That's where we're going," Ellie explained.

Great. We were going to have to wander through the forest at night again. That was definitely not my favorite thing. Even though this forest wasn't particularly scary - in fact, old spirits called Hotaru came out when it was dark and gave light to mark the way - I still wasn't a huge fan. Maybe it was because I'd seen too many Forbidden Forest scenes in the *Harry Potter* movies.

Instead of following the path that Ellie and I had taken the other day, we quickly cut to the right and followed a new, unfamiliar path for about a mile. Eventually, we reached a clearing, about half the size of a football field, where sure enough, a large, white tree with golden leaves that grew from the branches. Around the tree, on wooden stakes were golden plaques, about a half dozen of them.

"Are those the grave markers for the elves that have died?" I asked, and Sara nodded.

"Have there really only been six elves from here who have ever died?" I asked, my mouth agape.

"That's right," Ellie said. "Lorondir is the first one in fifty years. Just after World War II there was a duel between another elf from Western Woods and one from the east, and the other elf won. That was the last time we had an elf death."

All around us were elves dressed in white robes - tall, solemn, and graceful.

"Do you see Farawir?" I asked, and Sara nodded. "He's over there." She pointed towards an elf who was rather on the shorter side compared to his brethren – only a touch over six feet tall – with black hair that reached just past his shoulders. His blue eyes were like steel; whether it was because he felt no guilt over killing his father or because he was simply holding in his grief, I wasn't certain.

"Next to Farawar is Lorondir's sister, Elawa. She's one of the ten female elves in town."

"Wow, there really aren't a lot of females, are there?" I asked. Elawa's eyes were red-rimmed; she had obviously been crying.

"No, not at all. Elawa works as a bookkeeper, which is basically the lowest job an elf can get, but she's quite friendly and bubbly – for an elf, anyway – most of the time," Ellie explained. "I know she and Lorondir were close – they had coffee every Wednesday morning before work at Hexpresso Bean, and she took care of him domestically, getting his groceries and doing his laundry, since Lorondir and his wife divorced hundreds of years ago."

I was only half-listening, my attention turned fully on to Farawir. He had moved away from his aunt now, and was making his way towards the white tree. He placed a single hand on it, and if I wasn't mistaken, a single tear fell from his eye and onto the ground below. A second later, he seemed to have composed himself, and he made his way back to his group.

As more and more people gathered around, I spotted Chief Enforcer King at the outside of the group. There were no chairs or anything; this was definitely different to the wizard's funeral I had attended less than a week earlier.

Slipping away from Ellie and Sara for a moment, letting them know I'd be back, I made my way towards Aria King. I hadn't seen her since I had gotten away from the murderer last time around, and I wanted to thank her.

"Chief Enforcer King!" I said, and she turned. With her long, copper-blonde hair and brown eyes, it was obvious from the start that Aria King was a lion shifter.

"Tina," she said with a smile. "How are things going? Are you healing up alright after last week?"

I nodded. "Absolutely. I didn't have more than a few scratches and some sore muscles for a few days."

"And Mr. Meowgi?"

"Thanks to Sara's mom, he's back to his normal self. Listen, I wanted to thank you for your help that day. It's good to know that the bad guy is behind bars."

"Absolutely, not a problem. Though in the future, I'd prefer it if you left the law enforcement to, well, law enforcement. And that includes this most recent murder," she said, motioning towards the white tree. "I know your friend Sara was the one taking Lorondir on her broom when he died, but that's no reason to be involving yourself."

"Oh, don't worry, we have no intention of investigating his murder," I lied, crossing my fingers behind my back. The look Aria gave me was one of total disbelief.

"Right. Of course you weren't. You just so happened to go to the law firm and speak with one of the lawyers there."

A blush crawled up my face. "Well, um, you know, while we didn't know if Sara was a suspect or not…" I stammered, my voice trailing off. I was definitely not great under pressure. Ellie would have come up with a smooth lie straight away, I was sure of that.

"I can tell you that at the moment, we haven't ruled

anyone out as a suspect completely, but that doesn't mean you can investigate yourself."

"Wait, but if Lorondir was poisoned, how could Sara have done it?"

"How do you know he was poisoned?" Aria asked, her eyes narrowing at me, and the blush in my face turned a deeper red. I was probably doing a pretty good tomato impression right about now.

"Sara may have accidentally overheard you telling one of the other Enforcers," I mumbled.

"Of course she did," Chief Enforcer King said. She didn't look mad; if anything she looked a little bit bemused. "Anyway, while the fact that Lorondir was poisoned may be correct, we are looking at anyone who had contact with him that morning as being a suspect, and eliminating them as quickly as we can."

"Did you know that his son, Farawir, has fallen back into a gambling addiction in the last month?" I asked. After all, seeing as Chief Enforcer King knew that we had been investigating, the least I could do was give her what information we had found out. The important thing was that the killer be discovered.

Chief Enforcer King raised an eyebrow. "Thank you for the information. As this is an ongoing investigation, I can neither confirm nor deny what I do or do not know, but I appreciate you telling me what you've discovered. I do hope this will be the end of your investigating."

I nodded meekly. "Right."

At least now we had confirmation of the poisoning. Someone had slipped something to Lorondir the morning of his death, going by what Chief Enforcer King said. Now we not only had a method of death, but also a bit more of a timeline.

CHAPTER 12

About five minutes after I left Chief Enforcer King and made my way back to my friends, the ceremony began. There was no pastor, or priest, or anything of the sort. Instead, about a dozen elves, including Lorondir's son and his sister, joined hands and made a big circle around the white tree. When they began chanting, the idle viewers like us stopped talking and spread out in a circle as well.

I couldn't make out the words they were saying; it was definitely a different language. Elvish, I supposed. Making a mental note to ask Amy what the elvish language was called, before I made yet another social faux-pas, I watched, riveted, as the song of the elves got louder and louder, their chanting rhythmic and calming. I found myself completely transfixed as the elves stood in their large circle, before suddenly they stopped, and Farawir stepped forward. He stood directly in front of the large white tree, and wordlessly, he knelt to the ground for a second, coming back up holding a large urn.

For a moment, Farawir whispered to the urn, then took off the top, dropped it on the ground, and held the urn above his head.

At that very instant the wind picked up, and a gust swirled around, almost like a miniature tornado, taking the ashes and lifting them up high, spreading them through the forest.

Amy had told me that elves had a kind of magic that was very connected to the earth, and I knew better than to imagine that gust of wind was in any way natural.

A final gust of wind whooshed over the head of the onlookers, and the elves all took a single large step back before turning away from the tree and making their way back over to the crowd.

It appeared the funeral – or whatever this ceremony was called – was over.

The crowd began to mingle once more, with everyone making their way over to the grieving elves. Ellie, Sara, and I joined in with them. After all, just because we had come here to get a look at Farawir ourselves – and to see if Jordan Black was here, although none of us had noticed him yet – didn't mean we couldn't pay our respects as well.

Eventually, we made our way towards the family. Farawir was the first we spoke to.

"Sorry for your loss," I said to him, my words earnest. I knew all too well what it was like to lose a parent, and I figured even if you were hundreds of years old, it wasn't easier. And I didn't *know* he was the killer; there was a chance it was Black.

"Thanks," he muttered, not looking me in the eye. "Appreciate it."

I moved on to Elawa, Lorondir's sister.

"I'm so sorry," I told her, and she clasped both my hands in hers.

"Thank you for coming. You're the new witch, aren't you?" I nodded in reply. "You would not have known my brother, but it means so much to me that you came all the same."

"Of course," I replied before moving on; there were a lot of people in this line.

"It was good of you to come," the man next to them said to me. "I echo my sister's sentiments." So this was Lorondir's brother.

"I only wish we could have met under better circumstances."

"As do I, dear witch. As do I."

After we passed through the crowd, the three of us made our way to the edge of the woods.

"That was a beautiful ceremony," Ellie said. "I'd never seen an elf funeral before."

"Do they use their language much, the elves?" I asked. "Is it called elvish?"

"Elfin," Sara replied. "And no, it's very ceremonial

these days. I think way back when they used to speak it regularly among themselves, but now they just stick to English like the rest of us. They'll still speak it if they really don't want to be eavesdropped on, though."

I nodded. That made sense.

"So what do we do now?" I asked. "Head back and wait for the invisibility potion to be ready?" I looked warily towards the woods. The sun had definitely set now, and the last glimmers of light were fast disappearing. I wanted to get out of here as quickly as possible.

"What was that?" Ellie asked suddenly.

"What was what?" I replied, looking into the woods instinctively.

"I saw something – someone – in the woods over there," Ellie said. "Follow me."

"Great," I muttered as Ellie stormed into the woods behind us, not the least bit worried about going into the creepy forest at night after some sort of mystery creature.

Sara followed in after her with only a split-second hesitation, and I sighed. I didn't want to gain a reputation as being the wussy one in the group. Then again, I also didn't want to get eaten by whatever random creatures lived in there.

Still, the fear of my peer's ridicule outweighing my fear of death – what was *wrong* with me? – I followed after Sara, hoping that we were just going after a deer or something.

"You! Stop!" I heard Ellie cry out from about fifty

feet in front of me. There was a commotion, then I heard Ellie's voice once more: *"Lightning cracks, and you stop in your tracks."*

A man's voice shouted in frustration, and as I caught up to the other two, I saw them walking towards a man who was definitely Jordan Black. He squirmed in place, obviously trying to move, but it was like his feet were cemented into the ground.

"What in the name of Nanook have you done to me?" Black growled, and the hair on my arms stood on end, even knowing that he was trapped by Ellie's spell.

"We need you to answer some questions. Then we'll let you go," Ellie said, her wand still pointed directly at Jordan Black. He let out a low growl.

"And why should I answer your questions?"

"Because otherwise you're going to spend a whole lot of time stuck here in this forest," Ellie said. "And remember, in running from me you veered pretty far off the path, so who knows how long it will be before someone else comes this way looking for you?"

Black looked from one of us to the other, and I tried to put on my most threatening expression. I probably looked like I was just trying to hold in some bodily functions instead, but oh well.

Eventually, realizing that there was no way he was going to get out of there without Ellie undoing the spell, he sighed. "Fine. What do you want to know?" He asked in his thick northern English accent.

"Did you kill Lorondir?" Ellie asked.

"What? No, of course I didn't."

"Well, it's not obvious to us. After all, he *did* get you convicted of murder."

"Nah, those twelve idiots on that jury did that. Lorondir put up a good defense."

"A good enough defense to get you convicted?"

Black laughed, but it was a dark and humorless laugh. "You don't get it, do you? Lorondir knew we were cooked. There were no two ways about it. They had so much evidence a freaking squirrel could have won that case. So he purposely screwed up. The man was a bloody brilliant lawyer, he managed it so no one noticed, and gave me instructions to give me new lawyer after I was convicted and had to appeal. And it worked! He was a brilliant elf. I'd never seen anything like it."

"Wait, so Lorondir *knew* he had screwed up?" I asked.

"Of course, it was his idea. And hey, it worked, he got me off."

"So why did you come here now?" Sara asked.

"I wanted to thank him. Two days ago was the final appeal the prosecutor could make to have my case re-evaluated, and they threw it out. I'm a free man forever, thanks to him."

Great. There went our motive, right out the window, if Black was telling us the truth.

As if she was reading my mind, Ellie said, "How do we know you're not lying about this?"

Black shrugged. "Have to take my word for it, I guess. But I'm telling you, I had no ill will towards Lorondir. I'm sad he's dead; it's why I came to his funeral today. I figured no one would really want to see me around here, so I hid in the forest, but I did want to see the ashes being released. He was a good elf. He was a much better elf than I am a shifter, if I'm honest."

"That really doesn't seem like that high a bar to clear," Ellie said, raising an eyebrow, and Black growled at her.

"Hey, I'm telling you what you want to know, aren't I?"

"Why did Lorondir destroy his reputation for you, though?" I asked. "I mean, it might have gotten you off the hook, but it also meant he looked like an idiot, and the guy did have a reputation to uphold."

"Oh, the old elf had been thinking about retiring for ages," Black said. "I think he did it in a way to reduce his workload. I guess he figured if people thought his legal mind wasn't what it used to be they'd look elsewhere, and he could sell his stake in his firm and retire."

"So who would have wanted him dead?" Ellie asked. "Got any thoughts on that?"

Black shrugged. "Wouldn't have a clue. This is my first time in Western Woods, and I don't know that he had any problems with anyone. Got along well with his siblings, and his son, from what I heard from him at the trial, but it's not like he gave me a list of people who were out to get him."

Ellie nodded. "Ok, thanks."

"Now, you gonna let me out of here?"

I could practically *feel* Ellie toying with the idea of leaving Jordan Black out here for the night, but eventually, she pointed her wand at him and cast the reversing spell, releasing him from the bonds.

"Bloody crazy witches," Black muttered. "I'm out of here." And without another word to any of us, he darted back into the forest, back towards Western Woods.

CHAPTER 13

"Well, if he's telling the truth, there goes his motive," I said as the three of us walked back towards the path that would lead us back to town. The Hotaru were out now, like little glowing fireflies guiding us back towards the path. In the darkness I was thankful for their spirits guiding us.

"I don't think he was lying," Sara said. "He seemed like he was telling the truth."

"I can believe that," Ellie said slowly. "After all, it was just *so* unlike Lorondir to really lose a trial like that and then have the verdict overturned on a technicality. He's been a lawyer for like, thousands of years. He knows the technicalities inside and out."

I nodded. "Yeah, I agree. I think Black was telling us the truth, which means that he's now off our suspect list, and we need to look at Farawir more closely."

"Good, because the potion should be ready, so we can go have a look in the law offices right now."

Half an hour later, the three of us made it home, and I opened the freezer door to discover, to my surprise, that the potion I had left had turned into a delightfully yummy looking shade of purple. It looked more like a smoothie than an invisibility potion.

Taking the cauldron out of the freezer and placing it on the table, Ellie nodded happily.

"Good, it looks perfect."

"So how does it work?" I asked.

"For every spoonful you take, you'll be invisible for a full hour," Ellie replied. "I don't think we'll be gone more than an hour, but we should play it safe and plan for two just in case."

"I agree," Sara nodded. "After the last time, when we almost got caught by the janitor, I definitely would rather err on the side of caution."

I nodded my agreement; using a potion to become invisible was definitely a good idea.

"Ok. Since the law office is just a couple blocks from here, I vote we walk instead of taking the brooms. It'll be easier."

"Agreed," Sara said, digging three tablespoons out from the cutlery drawer and handing them to me. While I had been made invisible with magic before, it had been with a spell, not a potion.

"Why aren't we using the spell again?" I asked, curious.

"Much like with anything else, every witch has her preferences and her skills. Amy prefers spells because she excels at them, while I've always been better with my hands than with a wand, so potions are more my thing."

"So do we take the potions and then meet there?" Sara asked.

Ellie nodded. "I think that's the best idea. We'll all go together, but if we get separated, we should meet at the rear entrance to the Law office."

"What about me?" Mr. Meowgi complained, jumping up onto the counter.

I had totally forgotten that I promised to take him with me the next time I went somewhere.

"You can come, but you have to stay out of sight. I don't think we can give you any of the potion," I said, looking over at Ellie with question marks in my eyes.

Ellie shook her head. "No, potions work slightly differently for animals than they do for humans."

"That won't be a problem," Mr. Meowgi said with a swish of his tail. "I have ninja-like skills when it comes to staying out of sight."

Resisting the urge to roll my eyes, I decided that it would probably be fine for him to come, even while visible. After all, cats were pretty well-known for being sneaky.

"Do you know where we're meeting?" I asked him.

"I do," Mr. Meowgi replied. "Don't worry about me.

If you let me out that front door I'll meet you at the rear entrance of that law office as well."

"Okay, but I'm telling you, if you get into any trouble you can't come with me again in the future," I warned as I made my way towards the front door and let Mr. Meowgi out.

"Says the witch who's about to do something totally illegal," Mr. Meowgi muttered as he darted out through the open doorway and into the night. His black coat was definitely good camouflage; within seconds I had lost track of him.

Making my way back to the kitchen, Sara handed me one of the tablespoons she had taken from the cutlery drawer, and gave the other one to Ellie.

"So, we all know the plan. Once we've taken a sip of the potion, we'll be able to hear each other, but we won't be able to see each other. Here goes nothing," Ellie said, dipping her spoon into the potion, and taking a sip.

Instantly, Ellie's curvy frame disappeared from view, and the only thing I could see was a mark in the potion as she dipped the spoon in for a second sip.

"Looks like it worked perfectly, as always," Sara said with an approving nod. "Good job."

"Thanks," Ellie said. It was weird hearing her voice as though she was standing right next to us - which, I supposed she was - but not being able to see her. "Who's up next?"

"I'll do it," I replied. Taking my spoon, I dipped it

into the bowl and came up with a heaping pile of smoothie-like invisibility potion. "Is this the right amount?"

"Sure is," Ellie said. "Besides, if you mess it up just a little bit, the only thing that happens is you stay invisible for a little bit longer."

Confident that the amount on my spoon wasn't going to screw something up, like turn me into a three-headed monster or anything, I held my nose just in case - I knew what ingredients had gone into this, and no matter how good it looked, I knew it shouldn't taste very good - and drank.

To my surprise, the potion didn't really have a taste, but it felt pretty fiery on the way down, like taking a shot of whiskey. It wasn't an altogether unpleasant feeling, and when I looked down a moment later, I couldn't see anything.

That was definitely weird; some of the spells I was definitely going to have to get used to. I poked with my invisible fingers where my legs should have been, and luckily, they were still there. I might have been invisible to the sight, but I was definitely still around.

"Have you taken your second spoonful?" Sara asked, and I shook my head before realizing a second later that she couldn't hear me at all.

"No, give me a sec," I replied, dipping my spoon into the potion once again and taking a second sip. "Okay, all good."

Sara nodded and repeated the same process as Ellie

and I had done. Instantly, she disappeared as well, and we were ready to go.

"We have two hours, ladies," Ellie said. "Sara, you know the drill, but Tina, just make sure when you're walking through town that you don't run into anybody. Otherwise, the game is up."

"You say Sara knows the drill? Is this a potion that you use regularly?"

Ellie laughed. "Not so much since we graduated from the Academy, but back in the day this potion came in really handy when we wanted to score some illegal herbs from the herbology storage room. Of course, because we always had professors around, we had to be careful not to run into them while we were running the potion. Otherwise the game was up."

"Let me guess, this was exclusively an Ellie and Sara thing, because Amy wouldn't have a thing to do with you guys?"

"You got it," Sara replied. "Ellie would make the potion, and then we would work together to get into the storage room."

I laughed; it was funny to hear how teenage antics existed regardless of species.

The three of us headed out, deciding to meet at the Law offices. After all, if we ran into anybody in town, we would easily get split up as we had no idea where the others were.

Yeah, there was definitely no way anything could go wrong. Not.

CHAPTER 14

"*W*here were you?" Mr. Meowgi asked accusingly as soon as I got to the Law office.

"Wait, you can see me?" I asked.

"Of course I can, your puny human potions are nothing compared to my superior feline instincts," Mr. Meowgi replied.

"Am I the only one you can see? Or can you see the others as well?"

"It's more of a sense than a see, to be honest," Mr. Meowgi replied. "But yes, I can sense Sara coming up behind us now."

"Hey, is anyone else here yet?" Sara asked in a soft voice.

"I am," I replied. "Hey, Mr. Meowgi says that he can sense where we are, even with the invisibility potion. Did you know that? Is that normal?"

"Yeah, it is," Sara replied. "That was why, at the Academy, even though we had the invisibility potion we had to be careful, because we didn't want any of the professors' familiars to notice us sneaking in to steal supplies."

I made a mental note to remember that, then scolded myself for even thinking about the fact that things like this could become a regular occurrence here. This was definitely an exception; we were only here because we needed to know who killed Lorondir to clear Sara's name.

"Hey," Ellie said. "Am I the last one to arrive?"

"Sure are," Sara replied.

"Sorry, there were a couple of vampires blocking my route, and I had to take a bit of a detour," Ellie replied. "I assume I'm the one doing the spell to check for wards?"

"I feel like that's safer for everyone," Sara replied. I had to agree with her; Sara's magic had a history of being, well, creative. The spells she used didn't always do what she expected.

Ellie muttered some words I couldn't make out, and all of a sudden, the back door to the building glowed a deep red color.

"Great, there is a ward on it, and the red means it's fairly advanced."

"Can you break it?" I asked.

"We'll see. This is the disadvantage to Amy working tonight; she's a lot better at this sort of thing than

I am."

I watched as Ellie muttered some more words, and then repeated the ward detection spell, but once again the door glowed red.

"I don't want to try too many times," Ellie said. "A lot of these wards are set up so that if you try to detect them too many times, an alarm is set off."

"A silent alarm?" I asked.

"Yeah. We won't know until all of a sudden one of the Enforcers show up to arrest us."

I bit my lip. "We have to get in there somehow." Making my way to the side of the building, I noticed a bunch of smaller windows.

"How do the wards work? If the door is opened from the inside, will they still activate?"

"No, they're only set to activate from the outside, generally," Ellie explained. "So if the door was opened from the inside, it would be fine. But of course, there's the question of how to get inside."

"I think Mr. Meowgi might be able to help us with that," I said with a grin I knew the others couldn't see. "Come over to the side of the building."

I heard the shuffling of a few steps as the others made their way over as I'd asked. "See those windows? Are they warded?"

"Let me check," Ellie said, muttering the same spell again. A few seconds later, they glowed blue. "Nope, no wards."

"Good. Mr. Meowgi, can you go in through the

window if we use an unlocking spell and then open the back door for us from the inside? I know it's hard since you don't have opposable thumbs."

"Please, I'm a cat. I'm inherently a more capable being than any of you."

"Right, other than the part where you don't have opposable thumbs," I muttered in reply as Ellie cast an unlocking spell on the window. A moment later, it was open.

"Watch and learn, witches," Mr. Meowgi announced, jumping straight up off the ground and onto the windowsill, and disappearing inside.

"Do you think he's going to manage it?" Ellie asked.

"For sure, his pride won't let him fail," I replied with a grin I knew the others couldn't see. I was quickly growing quite fond of my snarky little familiar.

The three of us went back around to the back door, and a couple of minutes later there was a click, and the door opened, Mr. Meowgi hanging off the handle with his front paws as it swung open towards us.

"You did it!" I said. "You saved the day, Mr. Meowgi."

Dropping to the ground and landing elegantly on all four paws, Mr. Meowgi calmly sat down and began licking one of them.

"I always told you I would," he said casually, as if he broke into office buildings and helped his witch get inside on a daily basis.

"You're the best," I said as the three of us slipped into the dark building.

"Ok, I think we should split up," I announced when we got inside. "After all, we're looking for a will that could be anywhere. It might be in Lorondir's office, it might be in someone else's office. I mean, it's even possible that the original isn't here anymore, since he's dead and all."

"Agreed. Besides, even Lorondir would have needed a different lawyer to sign off on the will. Lawyers can't sign their own documents when a lawyer's signature is required," Ellie said.

"Ok. We meet back here in say, forty-five minutes and see what we've got?"

"Sure," Sara said.

I took my wand out from my back pants pocket. I had learned this spell with Amy; it was the only spell I really knew how to do. I focused my energy on my wand, trying my best to make the wand feel like an extension of my body. The energy built up inside of me, my magical energy I now knew, and I focused it on the wand.

"*Jupiter, with all your might, I beseech you to fill this room with light,*" I announced, and the tip of my wand glowed white, giving off about as much light as my phone's flashlight would have.

"Not bad, for a witch from a different coven," Ellie's voice called out from down the hall, and I smiled.

"Thanks!" Because we didn't know which coven I

belonged to, I had to use the spells from this coven, which didn't work as well as they would for someone who actually did belong to the coven of Jupiter.

Ellie did the spell as well, and her wand emitted a much brighter glow than mine. Then Sara repeated it as well, and to my surprise, her spell actually worked. Her glow was slightly brighter than mine, although not much, and certainly less bright than Ellie's glow.

"Good job," I told her with a nod.

"This is the one spell I can actually usually do without anything going wrong," she explained. "It's probably why Amy chose it as the first spell for you to learn; she probably figured that if even I could do it, then there was no way for you to mess it up."

The three of us split up; I could tell where the others were now thanks to the light emitting from our wands. Making my way down the hall, Sara tried the door to Lorondir's office. Locked.

"Can you check for a ward and unlock this for me?" Sara asked Ellie.

"Sure," Ellie replied. "I doubt there will be wards in here, but you never know."

A few seconds later it was confirmed that the door wasn't warded, and Ellie unlocked it for Sara.

"How about you, Tina? Where do you want to look, since I'll have to unlock that door as well?"

Next to Lorondir's office was the one which belonged to Manarwa, who Amy and I had visited the other day. She had seemed close to Lorondir, and she did say she was a civil lawyer, so maybe he would have used her to do his will? Plus, hadn't Maria said that Lorondir spoke to "the female elf" about his will? That had to be Manarwa.

"How about this one?" I asked, and Ellie nodded, repeating the spells. The door clicked open, and I slipped through, thanking Ellie, who said to find her if I needed anything else unlocked.

I was in.

CHAPTER 15

Manarwa's office looked a lot creepier in the middle of the night, with the small light from my wand casting shadows everywhere.

I immediately made my way to the file cabinet on the side, and wasn't surprised to find it was locked. However, Manarwa being an elf and not a witch, I had a feeling that this wasn't a magical lock, and sure enough, in the top desk drawer I found a key which unlocked it, saving me from interrupting Ellie.

As I scanned through file after file, I quickly found my eyes glazing over. How on earth anyone managed to find being a lawyer interesting, I would never know. Manarwa seemed to mainly deal in corporate law and contracts; there were a ton of files about building permits, contracts, land parcel transfers, and that sort of thing.

It was comforting in a way, to see that even in the magical world, red tape was definitely a thing.

As time passed and my boredom level grew, so did my frustration level. There was nothing in any of the files relating to Lorondir, and I hoped that the others had had more luck than I did in finding something – anything – related to his will.

Putting everything back exactly as I'd found it, I sat back on my haunches and wondered what the next move was. There were still twenty minutes to go before I had to meet the others by the back door again, so I could probably check someone else's office.

As I went to put the key to the cabinet back where I had found it, however, something caught my eye. In that same drawer was a single manila envelope, and when I opened it, I found exactly what I was looking for.

Last Will and Testament: Lorondir of the Elves

Sitting in Manarwa's chair, I pulled everything from the envelope and placed it on her empty desk. Looking more closely, there were in fact, two copies of the will. I flipped to the end to find that they were dated differently, however.

One of the wills was dated less than a week earlier. The other, however, was dated March 17th, 710 *Ab urbe contida*.

"When on earth was that?" I muttered.

"Hey, do any of you know what 'ab urbe contida' means?" I shouted out into the hall.

"It's how they used to calculate years a long time ago," Ellie shouted back. "What year exactly?"

"710."

"Hold on, let me do some napkin math." A moment later, she called out again. "44 BC in our years."

My eyes widened. Lorondir's last will had been made two days after Julius Caesar had been assassinated.

Raising an eyebrow slightly, I turned to the contents of the will.

The new will left everything to Farawir, Lorondir's son, as we had suspected. Farawir did inherit everything, which gave him an excellent reason to want his father dead, especially if he was getting in over his head with the gambling stuff once again.

The older will, the one that had been in place for over two thousand years – geez, elves led crazy lives – had left everything to Elawa, Lorondir's sister. A note on the front of the new will said that a copy had been left at the post office to take to Elawa on Monday. Since Lorondir had been killed on Wednesday, that meant Elawa knew that she was no longer in the will. A note also mentioned that the same notice was given to Farawir; he would have known that he inherited his father's estate when Lorondir was killed.

This confirmed Farawir's financial motive: if he needed the money, and was desperate enough for it, he would have known that he could have killed his father for it.

"Hello? Who's there?" a voice suddenly called out from the hallway. I froze, my eyes widening. It definitely wasn't Ellie or Sara's voice, this was a man.

"I know you're out there," the man said. "Come on out."

I dropped my wand in surprise, and the light immediately went out. That was definitely a good thing; someone knew we were here and as long as I stayed quiet, maybe there was a chance that they would go away.

Making my way to the doorway, I went to have a look at the person who had come in. How did they know we were here? Had we messed up one of the spells on the wards? Or maybe we had triggered one without realizing it.

At the far end of the hallway, carrying a flashlight, was a vampire. His pale face, dark hair, and fangs gave it away. And on top of all that, he had that creepy vampire look about him that made a chill run up my spine. This guy just looked like bad news.

He made his way towards where I was, sweeping his flashlight back and forth. He flared his nostrils and sniffed, as though he could smell us. Could he smell us? From what I knew in the human world about vampires I didn't think they had that ability, but I had learned a lot about just how wrong I could be when it came to those sorts of things.

He came closer and closer to the doorway where I stood, and I knew that if he did have the ability to sniff me out, I was definitely caught. Great. I didn't know what jail time was for breaking and entering here, but I figured it probably wasn't super lenient.

On top of that, I really didn't want to get arrested in my first couple of weeks here in the paranormal world. I figured it probably wouldn't be a great first impression. I was just starting to regret deciding to come along on this trip, when all of a sudden I heard another familiar voice.

"Hey, Anton, you in here?"

"Kyran?" the vampire called out, and I inhaled sharply as I realized from the proximity of his voice that he was just outside the door.

"Yeah, man, what are you doing?"

"Someone triggered one of the wards in here, so I had to come check it out. Was it you?"

"Probably. I always forget where they all are. Sorry."

"What are you doing in here this late anyway?"

"I got a new lead on one of the people Manarwa wanted me to find. Can't tell you more than that, sorry. But anyway, I figured I'd come here and get the documents I need in case I catch him."

"Right. Well, at least that killed ten minutes. Try and be more careful about the wards, hey?"

"Will do, sorry man. My bad. Take care."

"Yeah, you too." I heard the vampire retreating, and a few minutes later, a door closed. The vampire was gone.

"So, do you witches want to come out and tell me what you're actually doing here?" Kyran called out.

"Sure," I replied. I stepped out into the hallway. "But unfortunately, you're not really going to see a lot of us."

Kyran burst out laughing. "Invisibility potion, huh?"

"How did you know that?" Sara asked.

"If you had done it with a spell, you could simply reverse it. Potions you need to wait until the effects wear off."

"How do you know that? You're an elf," Ellie said.

Kyran shrugged. "In my line of work, the more you know about all different types of paranormals, the less danger you're in. Anyway, what are you three doing here?"

"I could ask you the same question," Ellie said.

"Sure, but you already overheard the answer. On the other hand, if you don't tell me, you're going to have to tell Anton instead. And Anton is pretty fang-happy."

I figured that was the vampire version of trigger-happy. "We're looking for a copy of Lorondir's will," I admitted. "We want to know if it's true that Farawir inherits everything, since with his recent fall back into gambling we thought that if he really does inherit, he had good reason to have his father killed."

"So you know about the gambling addiction then," Kyran said, with an impressed nod. "That's some pretty good detective work."

"His father didn't know, though, did he?" I asked.

"No, he didn't. Not as far as I know, anyway. If he had, he would have changed the will back immediately."

"Do you know where the will is?" I heard Ellie's voice say. "I haven't found it."

"I did," I said, running through a summary of everything I had discovered.

"So our theory was correct," Sara said. "Farawir inherits, and he would have known since the owls would have sent notice."

"Owls? Your post office is run by owls?" I asked, always pleased when I discovered another similarity between *Harry Potter* and my new real life. "Can I send a howler to someone?"

"What on earth is a howler?" Ellie asked.

"Never mind," I mumbled. "You should read some of those books that I brought over from the human world, though."

"Anyway, yeah, the post office here uses owls to send letters and documents between people. It's more efficient than sending witches, and cheaper too, since owls don't have labor laws that apply to them."

I dreamed of going up to the post office, which I was from here on in going to refer to as the owlery, no matter what. But before I could finish my daydream, Kyran interrupted.

"So can I take it the three of you are leaving now?"

"Yeah, we can leave," I replied. "Thanks for covering for us."

"Hey, I recognize a righteous breaking of the law when I see one," Kyran grinned, and a blush crawled up my face. "I'll see you later. Try not to set off any more wards on your way out."

With that, Kyran turned and left, waving a hand behind him as he headed out the front door.

"Ok, fine, I'll admit it was nice of him to come and rescue us," Ellie said.

"It was," I agreed. "We would definitely be in jail right now if it wasn't for him."

"Let's get out of here," Sara said. "Now that we have what we're looking for, I don't want to be in here for any longer than we have to be."

"Where's Mr. Meowgi?" I asked, looking around. My familiar had evidently completely disappeared.

The three of us began searching for the cat, and I finally found him in what looked like a break room towards the back door. "In here," I called out to the others, as I made my way towards my familiar.

His face was fully inserted inside a bag of cat treats; he had managed to open one of the cupboard doors and get at the goodies which had probably been for the familiar of someone else working here.

"Come on, fatty, it's time to stop eating and to get going," I said to him, gently easing his face out of the bag and checking to make sure there were still treats in it.

"Hey, I need the calories for energy. It's hard work being a martial arts expert."

"Right, I'm sure your enemies will be terrified when you start rolling towards them," I replied. Mr. Meowgi scowled at me in response. "Anyway," I continued, "we have to go."

"Did you find what you were after?" Mr. Meowgi asked.

"We did, yes," I replied with a nod. I heard footsteps coming towards me, and then heard Ellie's voice.

"Not a second too soon, the potion is about to wear off in about five minutes."

Yup, this was our cue to get going.

CHAPTER 16

"*I* can't believe the three of you did that," Amy scowled when we got home and told her what we had discovered.

"You can't believe that we did it, or you can't believe that we did it without you?" Ellie asked with a grin.

"I can't believe you did that! Of course there were extra wards you can't detect there; lawyers aren't idiots. They might be elves, but they know security."

"Hey, at least Kyran was there to bail us out," I replied with a shrug.

"That's another thing. That guy's bad news, and you shouldn't be hanging out with him."

"It's not like we knew he was there," Sara replied. "Besides, you wouldn't have come with us anyway."

Amy crossed her arms. "Sure, but only because I actually understand the importance of attorney-client privilege."

Ellie grinned. "Amy wishes she was a lawyer," she said. "I can tell!"

"What? That's ridiculous," Amy replied. "I'm a witch. I can't be a lawyer."

"That's the stupidest rule," I chimed in. "Everything in this town is so segregated. Why doesn't everyone hang out together?"

"It's just not the done thing," Amy said.

"Are all paranormal towns like this?" I asked.

Sara nodded. "Yeah, pretty much. I mean, it makes sense in a way. You hang out with your own kind and that way things are a lot more peaceful."

I shook my head. "It doesn't have to be like that though. I mean, there are so many things that we could learn from other paranormal species. I don't think we should reject the idea out of hand just because that's how it's always been done."

I knew I was new in town, but I also knew I was right. After all, I was sure there was a lot we could learn from vampires, or fairies, or elves. And I didn't think that people should be pigeonholed into a certain job just because of their species of paranormal.

"Anyway, we're getting off topic," Ellie said. "We found the will, and Farawir had to know he inherited. The will was changed days ago and he was given notice."

Amy nodded slowly. "Okay, so that's that. I assume Chief Enforcer King knows this, though. After all, she's investigating a murder."

"I would think so," I said. "Assuming that what Jordan Black told us was true, and for what it's worth I think he was telling the truth, that leaves Farawir as the main suspect. Plus, he had the opportunity as well, since he had a meeting with his father that morning just before Lorondir died."

"So basically, it's time to leave things to Chief Enforcer King," Amy said. "After all, this means Sara is no longer really a suspect, so we have no reason to keep investigating. Plus, Chief Enforcer King is going to know all of this, and so if Farawir really did do it, she'll arrest him."

I had to admit, Amy's words made sense.

"Fine," Sara said. "I think Chief Enforcer King will do the right thing."

Ellie's face fell slightly. "Can't we just keep investigating for fun?" She asked. "After all, the last time we did this we ended up finding a murderer."

"Yes, and Tina and Mr. Meowgi both almost died," Amy replied, shooting Ellie a look.

"Yeah, but they didn't, and this time we'll be ready for them," Ellie said, but going by the expression on Amy's face, she definitely did not agree.

"I think until anything changes, Amy's right," I said. "I think we should leave this to the professionals for now."

"Fine, you guys are no fun," Ellie said.

"Seeing as fun almost got us thrown in jail tonight, I'm okay with that," I replied with a smile.

"But again, if anything changes, I'm willing to change my mind."

Little did I know just how soon that was going to happen.

~

"*H*ave things always been like this?" I asked Mr. Meowgi as we hung out in our room later that night. It was late, and with Ellie and Sara having to work in the morning, the three of us quickly went to bed after our discussion. Still, I couldn't get the idea of the segregation here in Western Woods out of my head. "You know, with all of the paranormals refusing to spend time with different species?"

"Yes, at least, so far as I know."

"Does it make sense to you?"

"Of course it does," Mr. Meowgi replied. "You don't see me hanging out with the dogs, or the owl familiars. They're just too different from me. They're a completely different species. What would we have in common?"

"How do you know, if you haven't spent any time with any of them?"

That got Mr. Meowgi thinking. "I suppose it's like in the movie *Rush Hour*. Initially, Carter and Lee didn't get along at all, because neither one of them thought they were anything like the other, but despite their differences they ended up becoming very good friends and partners."

"Yes, exactly like that," I said. I had forgotten that Mr. Meowgi had actually spent a decent amount of time in the human world before he was called to be my familiar, and that he had seen a number of human-world martial arts movies.

An idea began to form in my head. It might have been a really stupid idea, but it was an idea all the same. I wanted to see the people in Western Woods working together, I wanted to see them getting along regardless of species, and I had a sneaking suspicion that this might start getting us there.

"Do you know if there's anywhere in Western Woods where I could get movies from the human world?" I asked Mr. Meowgi.

"Not that I know of," he replied. "You might be able to go to one of the bigger paranormal towns, and they might have one of those niche stores that sell novelty items that come from the human world, but that would be it. Other than that, your best bet is to go back to the human world yourself and get them."

I frowned. For what it was worth, I actually had no desire to go back to Seattle. This was my home now, and I wanted to treat it that way.

"Why do you ask? Do you miss Jackie Chan movies?"

"No, I was thinking it might be a good way to get everybody together. Maybe I could organize some sort of human movie night, where I invite all of the paranormals in to the coven gardens to watch a movie. After all, movies bring people together. Maybe if everyone sees them, they'll come to realize that they're not all so different and maybe this rift between all the different types of paranormals here can be slowly eradicated."

"You're a weird witch, you know that?" Mr. Meowgi said. "Why can't you just stick with the status quo?"

"Because the status quo limits people. And I think that's wrong."

"Fair enough," Mr. Meowgi said. "Is there anything I can do to help?"

"I don't think so. Not yet, anyway. I'm not 100% sure if this is going to work, or how it's going to work, but if I think of anything for you to do, I'll let you know."

As I lay down in bed, turning off the light, I sat there awake. It really bothered me the way all the paranormals here in Western Woods treated each other, and I swore I was going to do my best to bring them all together just a little bit.

CHAPTER 17

The next morning, I sat at the table eating a bowl of cereal for breakfast, wondering if I should sprinkle on some golden flakes labelled 'energy' that were in the pantry. After all, I had only slept for about five hours, my head was pounding, and my brain felt like it was in a permanent fog. I was definitely going to have to make it to Hexpresso Bean later on to get a coffee.

Eventually, I decided against the flakes - after all, I had absolutely no idea how many to put on, or even if they would do what I thought they would do, and I figured playing around with magical food that I didn't understand was probably not the greatest idea ever.

Just as I was finishing up and putting my empty dishes in the sink, Amy made her way into the kitchen.

"What's up?" I asked her as she went to the fridge and grabbed a pile of grapes.

"I have the day off today, so I was thinking I would go to the library and do a little bit of extra studying," Amy said. "Then, I realized that I could spend the day teaching you a new spell, and I really wanted to explore the effect of water on your magic skills, so I think we'll do that instead. Sound good?"

"Sure," I nodded. I was always happy to learn more magic, especially since I knew just how much I still had to catch up on.

"Let me have a quick breakfast, and then we'll get started."

As soon as I opened the front door, Mr. Meowgi ran out, evidently happy to go on whatever adventures cats came up with.

"Don't go too far, and don't eat any wildlife," I yelled after my cat.

"Sure thing, boss," he replied as he darted away, and I smiled. Mr. Meowgi had a lot of energy, which was nice. Amy and I walked around the side of the house, which still had a few bushes along it before we reached the back of the house, which was now a giant pool, with just a couple of feet of tile between the water and the house.

"Great," Amy said as we made our way towards the edge of the water. "Are there any spells that you would like me to teach you?"

I shook my head. "Honestly, not really. I mean, I see everything that you manage to do with magic, and it seems a little bit overwhelming at times. Plus, I don't know what the easiest spells to do are, and you do."

Amy nodded. "Okay, I want to teach you two spells today. One of them will be calling on water, and the other will not be water related, but I want to see whether there is any change to how you perform the spell when you are in the water."

"Sounds good," I said, pulling out my wand. I was definitely getting used to carrying it around, and my wand was finally starting to feel like a part of me.

"Now, the first spell I want to teach you is one to call on water. This is of course, a Jupiter based spell, but I suspect you will be better at performing it then you would be a non-water related spell. Repeat after me, and remember to really feel the energy passing through your wand. *Jupiter, God of thunder, use my wand and bring forth water.*"

Amy pointed her wand towards the middle of the pool, and water suddenly spurted out of the tip, like she had just opened a fire hydrant. I took a step back at the sheer force of the water coming from her wand.

"Woah," I said, my eyes widening. Amy was definitely amazing at magic.

"Now, you try," Amy said. "Do you remember the words?"

I nodded as I closed my eyes for a second and focused on my wand. I imagined my wand as an extension of my body, and imagined all of the energy inside of me heading towards it.

"*Jupiter, God of thunder, use my wand and bring forth water,*" I said, feeling the energy inside of me build up. Suddenly, from the tip of my wand came a decent stream of water. It certainly wasn't as strong or powerful as Amy's had been, but it also wasn't a slow drip, either.

"Good, that's actually really good," Amy said, nodding contentedly. "I think the fact that you're a witch from a coven of water is definitely helping."

"What if I were to try a spell from a random water coven?" I asked. "After all, would it work better if I used the spell from the coven of Pluto, even if I'm not from that coven?"

Amy nodded. "That's an excellent idea. I don't know the spells for any of the other covens, but I can look them up at the library, and we can see what effect they have on your magical powers. Who knows? The odds are incredibly slim, but it's possible that we may even accidentally discover which coven you do belong to."

I couldn't help the smile that crept onto my face at that sentence. I tried not to think about it too much, but a part of me really wondered what coven I had come from. I wondered who my parents were - my biological parents, anyway - and why they had abandoned me. I thought that maybe if I discovered which coven I had come from, I'd be able to get the answer to all of those questions.

"Now, I also want you to learn the opposite spell: you're going to learn how to create fire."

"Cool," I said with a grin. After all, this actually did sound a lot more awesome than being able to make a bit of light or water appear out of nowhere. Being able to create fire with my wand was basically the equivalent of becoming a human flamethrower, like one of the X-Men.

"Now, of course, when you're doing this spell, make sure that you point your wand towards the sky. We don't want any major accidents."

I nodded and watched as Amy pointed her wand upwards. "*Jupiter, bring forth fire, the cousin of Lightning.*"

Straight away, a burst of flame erupted from Amy's wand and made its way hundreds of feet into the air. I gasped, impressed. That was way more than I had ever imagined. A second later, Amy ended the connection with her wand, and the flames disappeared. "Now, your turn."

Knowing that there was no chance that my fire was ever going to be as big as Amy's, I was still a little bit nervous as I pointed my wand towards the sky, being extra careful that it wasn't going to hit anything. After all, there was a large tree about 100 feet away, and I made sure my flame was definitely not in its path.

"*Jupiter, bring forth fire, the cousin of Lightning,*" I said, focusing my energy towards my wand once more. This time, unlike Amy's spell, mine just shot out a little bit of a flame. It honestly wasn't much more useful than a barbecue lighter, and I had to admit, I was pretty disappointed.

I had a feeling my emotions were written all over my face, because Amy smiled at me nicely. "Don't worry, it wasn't that bad."

"Yeah, but yours was just way better," I replied.

"You keep forgetting that these are the spells of my coven, and not of yours. I didn't expect you to do much, and the fact that you were able to create any fire at all is impressive by itself."

"Still, I was hoping that my flame would've been a little bit more… well, deadly."

"Let's see if it is when you put your feet in the water," Amy said, motioning to the pool that took up the entire backyard. "Take off your shoes and socks, dip your feet in the water, and try the spell again. We're going to see what happens when you do that."

I did as Amy asked, sitting on the edge of the pool and letting my feet drop in. The cool water was nice; even though it was only just after nine in the morning, the day was already starting to heat up. I took my wand once more and focused my energy, repeating the spell.

This time, rather than a flicker of a flame, the fire that came from the tip of my wand was a lot more explosive. The flame was about three feet long, and maybe a foot wide. As I broke the connection with my wand, I grinned at Amy. That was much, much better.

Amy nodded pensively. "Well, with that, I think we can say with 100% certainty that you are in fact a witch from a water coven. There is absolutely no way that you would have been able to generate a flame which was that much stronger without the water."

"So anytime I cast a spell, if I'm standing in water it will be stronger?" I asked.

"Yes, exactly," Amy replied. "For those of us from the coven of Jupiter, being in the midst of a thunderstorm has the same effect. Our powers are strengthened in that situation, because we are a coven of lightning."

I nodded slowly. I had to keep this in mind; it meant that I was stronger in water than in any other situation. In a way, I supposed it made sense. I had always been a strong swimmer; when my parents had signed me up for swimming lessons as a kid, everyone had been surprised at how strong a swimmer I was almost immediately, and I had actually joined the local swim club and won a few races before deciding I didn't really want to be an athlete.

"So if I try that first spell again as well, that will be stronger too?" I asked.

Amy nodded. "It should be, yes."

I pointed my wand towards the bushes at the side of the house. After all, it was a hot day, and I wasn't sure when the last time they had been watered was.

"*Jupiter, God of thunder, use my wand and bring forth water.*" This time, the water that shot out of my wand was practically like a water cannon. It was very similar to the amount of water which had come out of Amy's wand when she performed the same spell, and I saw her eyes widen in surprise and admiration as the water absolutely doused the plants. I really hoped I hadn't overdone it and damaged the plants; I hadn't expected the water coming out of my wand to be this powerful.

To my surprise, the plants let out a huge shriek. No, it wasn't the plants. A small, black figure darted out from underneath the bushes, water dripping as it ran as fast as it could towards me.

"What on earth is wrong with you?" Mr. Meowgi asked, glaring at me. He was completely soaked, running around as if he was trying to get the water off of him.

I couldn't help it; I burst out laughing. "What on earth were you doing in there?"

"I thought I saw a mouse."

"I thought I told you not to hunt any animals."

"You can't just turn off instinct. Now, do something to dry me off."

I looked over at Amy, helplessly. "I can't, I don't know how to do a drying spell."

"Stand still for a second," Amy ordered. Mr. Meowgi did as she asked, glaring over at me as he shivered in place, water still dripping off his fur. It was going to take a while before he forgave me for this.

"*Jupiter, with your power in the sky, use it now and make this cat dry.*"

Pointing her wand at Mr. Meowgi, his fur instantly went from completely soaked to bone dry.

"Oh, thank goodness. Tell that other witch that she

is much more powerful than you and that I like her more."

"Mr. Meowgi wants you to know that he likes you more than me," I said to Amy with a smile on my face, and she laughed.

"You're welcome," she said to my cat.

"That'll teach you to try hunting mice," I replied. "If you can't be trusted not to harm the wildlife out here, I'm going to have to put you on a leash, like a dog."

"You wouldn't dare!" Mr. Meowgi gasped.

"Then instinct or not, behave yourself in the future," I said, shooting him a warning look. Amy's phone buzzed, and she interrupted as she read the text.

"Tina, we have to go back to the Law office. Sara just texted me. They just fired her for being a suspect in Lorondir's murder."

CHAPTER 18

*W*hen we got to the offices, less than fifteen minutes later, after dropping a still-irate Mr. Meowgi off in the house, we found Sara at the front of the building, tears streaming down her face. Her broom hung limply at her side, and my heart broke for her. She had been so proud of herself for being able to get a job, and now it was all gone.

"Tell us what happened," Amy said as soon as we reached her, taking her friend into a huge hug.

Sara sniffed. "It was awful. Absolutely awful. I don't want to talk about it."

Amy and I shared a look. This was obviously not good, but we needed to know exactly what had happened.

"Okay, come on," Amy said. "We're going to Hexpresso Bean, since you could definitely use a coffee that will dull the pain just a little bit."

Sara nodded mutely and followed after us as we led her way from the Law office that had just fired her. She left her broom at the front of the coffee shop, and the three of us went in, with Amy headed to the counter to order us food and drinks, while I led Sara to a quiet corner, motioning for her to sit down on an over-stuffed arm chair while I sat at one end of the couch next to her.

"Oh, Tina, I can't believe they did it," Sara said, the look on her face one of total dejection. "They actually fired me."

"Hey, listen, it's going to be okay, you hear me?"

Sara shook her head. "How on earth am I going to tell my mom what happened? I had finally gotten a job, and it was a good job. I mean sure, I wasn't a Healer the way she had always hoped I would be, but at least this job involved using my magic in the way I know best. And now it's gone."

"Don't worry about that for now," I said. "Here comes Amy now, can you tell us everything that happened?"

Amy sat down next to me on the couch, and Sara took a deep breath before starting her story.

"I came into work this morning, and Manarwa, who was one of the elves who bought out Lorondir's share of the firm, called me into her office. She said that while the investigation was still ongoing, they couldn't have anybody who was suspected of Lorondir's murder working for the firm. She said that it didn't look good for the company, and that they needed to make changes until everything was all sorted out."

"Oh, that's just awful," I said, reaching over and putting a hand over Sara's. I felt so bad for her; she had been so proud of getting this job and now it was all gone because of something that she hadn't done.

"Wait, but does that mean that when the murder is solved you'll be able to get your job back?" Amy asked.

"I guess so, but I mean, how long is that going to take? And in the meantime, I'm going to be known as the girl who lost her job because her boss died on her broom, and she was one of the suspects in his murder. That's not exactly the kind of reputation I want to have around here."

I could understand that. After all, right after I had entered Western Woods, someone had been murdered and a decent number of people in town thought that I had done it.

Amy looked at me. "So basically, we need to make sure that someone is arrested for this murder as soon as possible."

I smiled slightly. "Is that you suggesting that we get involved in this?"

"Hey, as much as I might think that it's a bad idea, Sara is obviously being railroaded here, and I'm not going to stand around and do nothing when she's had this job taken from her unfairly."

"You guys are the best friends I've ever had," Sara

said, more tears streaming down her face. "Thank you so much."

"Of course, it's the least we can do," I said. "Come on, drink your coffee and then we'll take you home so you can sleep it off for a bit while Amy and I take care of everything."

After all, we already had a pretty good idea of who had committed the murder. We just had to make sure that Chief Enforcer King knew about it as well. Sara was going to have her job back in no time.

After drinking the coffee, Sara looked noticeably perkier. The magic had obviously worked, but Amy and I still walked her home and made sure she was settled on the couch with a pint of ice cream and her favorite magical TV show to watch before heading off.

Amy and I left soon afterwards, making our way to Chief Enforcer King's office. When we got to the large building that housed most of the town's main administrative offices, we were met by a tall shifter with a long nose and stubbly grey beard. This guy had to be a wolf shifter.

"Who are you here to see today?" he asked as Amy and I entered the large, dark space.

"We need to see Chief Enforcer King," Amy replied. "It's extremely important."

"I'm afraid the Chief Enforcer is not taking visitors today," the wolf replied.

"I promise you, she wants to hear what we have to say," Amy said.

"Well, why don't you tell me what it is, and I'll decide whether or not it's important enough for you to see her."

Amy shook her head. "Sorry, it's private and confidential, and definitely far above your pay grade."

I had to smile; it appeared Amy could definitely have attitude when she wanted to.

The wolf shifter snarled at her. "Well, I'm afraid in that case I can't allow you to see her."

"That's alright," Amy said. "Can I have your name though? I would like to tell Chief Enforcer King exactly who it is who is preventing her from arresting a murderer in this town because he took his gatekeeping duties far too seriously."

The wolf looked around, as though there might be somebody around who could help advise him as to how he could get out of this mess. He began to size Amy up, trying to decide whether or not she really knew what she was talking about, or if she was just blowing smoke to try and see Chief Enforcer King.

Finally, he decided that we must have been telling the truth, or at least that it was in his best interest to believe that we were.

"Fine, follow me."

I grinned at Amy as the two of us followed after the wolf, who took off down the hall at such a rapid pace that I struggled to keep up with him without jogging. I knew exactly where Chief Enforcer King's office was, and when we were led into it, I found the lion shifter behind her desk, just finishing up a phone conversation. She held up a finger indicating that she needed a minute, then motioned for Amy and I to sit down on the two chairs in front of her.

"Right, got it. Thanks," Chief Enforcer King said with a nod, before hanging up the phone and facing Amy and I. "Good morning, witches. What can I do for you this morning?"

I decided to let Amy take the initiative on this one. After all, she was a lot better at this sort of thing that I was, and having been a lifelong resident of Western Woods would better know how to frame what we wanted to say.

"I'm not sure if you've heard, but Sara Neach was fired from her job this morning at Lorondir's law firm," Amy started.

"Oh, I'm so sorry," Chief Enforcer King said. "How awful."

Amy nodded. "Absolutely. It was all because the firm decided that they didn't want someone who is currently under investigation for murder to be working for them, as it looks bad."

"Well, I would love to help, but unfortunately that is their right," Chief Enforcer King said, opening her hands and shrugging.

"I know that, of course," Amy continued. "However, we thought that in the interests of having the guilty party brought to justice as quickly as possible, Tina and

I would come here and tell you who we think committed this crime."

Chief Enforcer King leaned back in her chair. "I thought that I had told Tina that you witches needed to stay out of this. Did she not pass on that message?"

"She did," Amy replied. "And I have absolutely not done anything since that conversation."

Technically, that wasn't a lie. After all, Amy had been working for Lita the night that the rest of us broke into the law firm and had a look at the will.

"However," Amy continued, "as you know, I do work for the head of the coven, and so as a result, I happen overhear a lot of conversation that happens within the walls of the coven headquarters, and I'm given the opportunity to speak with many of our esteemed citizens. The other day, I was told by a source that I trust that Lorondir changed his will in the week before his death, naming Farawir as his heir. We have also been told by someone who would know that Farawir has recently fallen back into the old gambling addiction that afflicted him in the past."

Chief Enforcer King studied the two of us for a while. "So the two of you are trying to tell me that Lorondir's son killed him."

I nodded. "That's what we think, yes. Have you had a chance to look at the will?"

A hint of a smile appeared on Chief Enforcer King's face. "That really isn't the sort of information I'm willing or able to tell civilians."

"Well, if you have, how come you haven't arrested Farawir yet?"

"Again, the sort of thing that I don't discuss with people who are not in law enforcement. But I can tell you this: I am extremely close to an arrest, and the information that the two of you have given me today should help me get a little bit closer to it."

Amy nodded. "You haven't been given access to the will, yet, have you?"

Chief Enforcer King looked at her with a shrewd eye. "You know a lot more about the law then you would like to admit, don't you?"

A blush crawled up Amy's face, and I recalled Ellie accusing Amy of wanting to be a lawyer. It made a lot of sense, and I imagined that Amy spent at least some of the time in the library reading about rules and regulations in Western Woods. After all, enforcing rules seemed to be exactly the sort of thing Amy would be excellent at.

"I know a little bit," Amy said. "In fact, the other day, I began to read up on the rules of inheritance, and I did find the law concerning the reading of wills in the cases of criminal investigations. Until the will is made public, without a reasonable belief that the contents of the will could be associated to the crime, the Chief Enforcer is not permitted to view the legal document before the rest of the paranormal citizenry."

Chief Enforcer King nodded, obviously impressed.

"You *do* know your stuff. You should have been born a shifter; you would have made an excellent Enforcer."

Amy's face flushed with pride for a moment.

"And don't think I don't know exactly why you came here," Chief Enforcer King said with a smile of her own. "Knowing this, you would have known exactly what you needed to tell me to give me access to the will before the public reading, a week from tomorrow."

I looked between the two women, impressed with both of them. Both Amy, for realizing what we had to tell Chief Enforcer King, and Chief Enforcer King for being able to see straight through Amy's plan.

"I don't know what you're talking about," Amy said, putting on a fake air of innocence. "I'm simply doing my duty as a citizen of Western Woods and telling the Chief Enforcer what I know about a crime which was committed in this jurisdiction."

"Of course you were," Chief Enforcer King said with a smile. "Can I trust that you will be willing to repeat what you told me in front of a magistrate?"

"Absolutely," Amy nodded. "Although if I am asked to reveal my sources, I am going to have to invoke the seventh article of the Paranormal Charter."

"Understood," Chief Enforcer King said. "I don't think it will come to that, though."

Amy stood up, and I followed her lead. The two of us shook hands with Chief Enforcer King, who thanked us once again, and Amy and I made our way back outside.

"I didn't realize that Chief Enforcer King wouldn't have gotten to see the will until now," I said as we left.

"That's because you don't study paranormal law," Amy said. "While a lot of it is similar to the human rules, there are certain aspects to our laws that are different. Don't worry though, the very few paranormals know about them as well; I wouldn't have known about the specific rule about wills if I hadn't been reading about them at the library after the three of you told me about the will."

"Well, it's a good thing you did. Now, hopefully Chief Enforcer King can get access to that will, and then she'll hopefully have the proof to arrest Farawir."

Chief Enforcer King was right: Amy would make an excellent enforcer.

CHAPTER 19

*W*hen we got back that afternoon, Amy and I decided not to tell Sara exactly what had happened in our discussion with Chief Enforcer King. After all, we didn't want to get her hopes up needlessly, just in case something went wrong and Chief Enforcer King didn't manage to arrest Farawir for his father's murder.

In the meantime, however, I set about my plan to start getting the paranormals of Western Woods to learn to enjoy each other's company regardless of species. I was definitely going to need some help, though, and I didn't want to tell my friends exactly where I was getting it.

"Hey, Mr. Meowgi, do you want to go for an adventure?" I asked my familiar.

"You don't have to say that word twice, I'm in," Mr. Meowgi replied.

"Where are you going?" Amy asked.

"I have a plan for a little bit of a party," I said. "But unfortunately, I need to get some stuff for it first."

"Really? What kind of party?" Ellie asked as she walked in through the door. "I love parties."

Looking at my friends, I realized that I definitely wasn't going to be able to keep this secret for long. And besides, a part of me really didn't want to, either. I figured I would tell them, although I wasn't mentioning what I was going out for, and see what their reaction was.

"I was going to host a party in the coven gardens for all different paranormal types," I said. "I want to show a famous human movie, something that maybe everybody can get a laugh out of and appreciate. I figure that maybe if everyone can come together and enjoy a movie, then maybe the paranormals here will realize that we're not all that different, and things might be able to change just a little bit."

"I actually think that's a really good idea," Sara said. "I would love to watch human movies with you, and I hope it works out."

"I can bake some food for it," Ellie suggested. "I'm not sure if it's going to do exactly what you want, but I'm happy to try for you."

"I don't think it will work," Amy said. "After all, there's a reason things have been the way they have been for thousands of years. The system we have now works, and I'm not sure that changing it is a good idea."

"Oh, come on," Ellie said. "You never know. I agree that this system we have now works, but that doesn't mean we should stop trying to improve it. Besides, nothing exciting ever happens here. Let's support Tina with this and see what happens."

"Fine," Amy said. "I'll come. When were you thinking of having this?"

"Would tomorrow be too early?" I asked. "I don't really know how to get the word out."

"We can take care of making sure all the witches know," Ellie said. "And I can make sure that the fairies know as well. Bluebell at the café knows absolutely every fairy in town, and so I can make sure she spreads the word to them."

"I would have said that I could tell the elves, but unfortunately that's not true anymore," Sara sighed. "I'll go to the hospital though, and get my mom to tell everyone she can."

"And I suppose I can spread the word among witches," Amy said.

I was actually so touched by my friends' support that tears welled into my eyes. "You guys are amazing," I told them. "I have to go source some stuff, but I'll be back later, okay?"

Mr. Meowgi and I left, my heart lightened with the knowledge that I had a few allies, even if they weren't completely on board with my opinions. They really were the best friends I could ask for.

"Do you really think it's going to work?" Mr. Meowgi asked. "Getting people together, I mean."

"I don't know," I shrugged. "I don't expect this movie night to change anything majorly in its own way, but I think if we can get a few paranormals together enjoying themselves for once, it might sow the seeds of something great in the future. After all, the only time I've ever really seen paranormals together was at funerals, and even then the same species seemed to hang out together."

"That's only natural, though," Mr. Meowgi said.

"No, that's not natural. There is no reason why a witch can't be good friends with a vampire, or why a fairy can't work as a lawyer, or anything like that. After all, we're all paranormals, and we should be embracing that similarity rather than discussing our differences."

"Well, I hope you manage to shake things up, but only because I'm a fan of drama. I don't particularly care what you paranormals do."

I grinned at Mr. Meowgi. "Good, because I need your help. I didn't want to tell the others where I was going, and I'm afraid I can't find The Bloody Mary by myself."

❧

I was careful to open the door as little as possible as I entered The Bloody Mary this time around, and the hissing from the patrons was a lot more muted than the last time I was here. Looking towards the counter, I was pleased to find the same bartender as the last time I was here.

"Great, the witch is back," he muttered. "I've already told you, I can't serve you here, and I don't want you coming around and bothering my patrons."

"Don't worry, I'm not here to talk anybody," I said. "I just wanted to ask you how I can find someone, and you seem like the kind of person that would know where to find him."

The bartender gave me the side eye, obviously not trusting me as he moved to the other end of the bar.

"What you want to know?"

"Where can I find the elf Kyrandir?"

"Why on earth would a nice witch like you want to know where he is?"

"That's my business. So, do you know, or not?" I replied, channeling my inner Ellie and trying to be more hard-core than I normally would have been.

"Yeah, I know where you can find him. If he's not in the human world, he'll be at the back of the club where the elves go, The White Tree."

"Thanks," I said with a nod.

"Now get out of here, and stop using me as a source for information. It doesn't look good for my business when I have witches in here."

"Fine, sorry," I muttered. "By the way, tomorrow I'm

hosting a human movie party in the coven gardens. It'll start just after sunset, if you want to let the vampires know they're all welcome."

"What movie is it?"

"Ummm," I started, realizing that I hadn't even decided on a film yet. The bartender gave me a strange look, and I spat out the name of the first movie that popped to mind. "*Spice World*."

Seriously? *Spice World*?

"What's it about?"

"A group of human girls who are pop stars," I muttered, slightly embarrassed. But hey, I had said we were going to watch *Spice World,* so I was kind of stuck with it now, wasn't I?

The vampire gave me a curt nod. "I won't make any promises."

Hey, that was better than nothing, right?

"Thanks," I said. "There will also be food, made by one of the cooks from Hexpresso Bean. Don't worry, I'm going now," I said, noticing the expression on the bartender's face was going back to annoyed. Mr. Meowgi and I slipped back out of the bar, and stood outside for a minute while waiting for our eyes to adjust back to the sunlight.

"I like it in there; it's nice and dark," Mr. Meowgi said. "Why can't witches appreciate a good night atmosphere?"

"Because nighttime is for sleeping," I replied. "Hey,

do you happen to know where The White Tree is? Apparently, it's the club where all of the elves have a tendency to hang out."

"Sure," Mr. Meowgi said. "It's in the forest."

Great. Of course it was.

CHAPTER 20

*M*r. Meowgi led the way deep into the forest, and while it was daylight and not nearly as creepy as that place was in the dark, it remained an incredibly thick forest that I was definitely not a fan of.

After about five minutes of following a single meandering trail, Mr. Meowgi and I arrived at a clearing that led to a small hill, into which was carved an open cave.

At the front of the cave stood a tall, robed elf with dark hair and eyes, who looked over at the two of us with an idle curiosity.

"You are here to meet somebody," the elf said, and I couldn't help but feel a shiver crawl up my spine. Elves had this magical ability to sense what other beings were feeling, and while it wasn't strictly mind-reading, it was still incredibly creepy.

"I would like to see Kyrandir, please," I explained, and the elf's eyebrows rose just slightly.

"I realize he probably doesn't get visitors often," I said.

"Please, follow me," the elf said, not replying to my comment. He turned and made his way inside the hole in the hill, and Mr. Meowgi and I followed after him. The interior of The White Tree was actually quite bright. Stained glass windows let in a lot of sunlight from outside, and candles along the wall were placed liberally, sending even more of a warm glow throughout the room.

I had a feeling that this place didn't actually serve alcohol; there was no bar, only large, comfortable seats surrounding small tables, with everything made of wood. The floor was wooden as well, as were the walls, but they were decorated with natural logs which gave the whole place a very woodland feeling. If we were back in the human world, this would've been a hipster's dream.

I couldn't help but notice that the eye of every elf in the room was trained on me. I felt incredibly out of place; this was obviously not a place that was regularly visited by witches. At least in the vampire bar none of the vampires seemed to really care that I had been there. The way the elves looked at me, you would think that I had invaded their sacred space.

Then again, for all I knew, maybe I had.

The elf led me to the very back of the room, where,

sitting in a chair with his back to everybody, sat Kyran. He had his phone out, and was busily typing away on it, but as soon as he saw me he stood up with a grin. The other elf stood for a second, bowed at me slightly, then turned on his heel and left without saying a single word to Kyran.

"Hey," Kyran said, motioning for me to sit down across from him. "What's up?" Mr. Meowgi jumped up onto Kyran's lap, and Kyran began stroking his fur, earning a purr of happiness from my familiar.

"I was looking for you," I said.

"I guessed that; I can't imagine why a witch would come in here for any other reason."

"I kind of got the impression it has been a while since any witch has been in here," I replied. "Don't tell me I just committed some kind of huge faux-pas."

Kyran grinned. "You definitely did, and I would know, I'm the King of faux-pas in this world."

"So I've heard."

"Come on, let's get out of here, so that the other elves in here stop shooting daggers at you."

He didn't have to ask twice. Kyran and I left the club, with Mr. Meowgi following hot on our heels. We walked into the forest, back along the trail towards town.

"So, what did you want from me?" Kyran asked.

"You go into the human world regularly, right?"

"Sure," Kyran nodded.

"I'm wondering if you'd be able to get me something."

Kyran smiled. "Missing stuff from home?"

"Not really. I mean, some things, yeah. But honestly, I've been so busy with learning to become a witch, and trying to find a couple of killers, that I haven't really had any down time since I've come here. But anyway, as I'm sure you know, this town has a pretty rigid hierarchy when it comes to how paranormals can interact with each other, and they seem to actively discourage mingling between paranormals of different species."

"I had noticed, yes," Kyran said, a casual smile flittering on his lips.

"Anyway, I've decided that's ridiculous, and I wanted to take a small role in fixing it."

"Really?" Kyran asked, raising an eyebrow. "And how exactly were you planning on doing that?"

"Well, I'm not about to do anything drastic or anything like that, but tomorrow I was going to organize a movie night in the coven gardens just after sunset, but I wanted to make it a human movie. After all, basically nobody here understands any of my references, so I figure human movies might be a nice novelty for the people here. I'm inviting all of the different paranormals, and while I don't expect an amazing turnout, I was thinking maybe if I make it a regular thing slowly more and more people might show up, and it might start changing people's attitudes."

I was expecting Kyran's reaction to be much like Ellie, Sara, and Amy's. Okay, maybe not Amy's. After all, she was much more in favor of keeping the status quo than Kyran, who was actively breaking it. I expected Kyran to tell me that it was never going to work, that no matter what the people here were set in their ways.

But to my surprise, he nodded.

"That's not a bad idea, actually," he said. "In fact, I think the fact that it might be small at first may work in your favor."

"Wait, you actually think this is a *good* idea?"

"I do," he replied. "You're right, of course, that the separation of paranormals in this town is ridiculous, and as you know I definitely don't agree with the hierarchy in jobs here. I don't think this is going to be some magical Band-Aid that will fix everything, but I think it's a step in the right direction, and I think Western Woods is lucky to have somebody like you who's willing to step out of the box that we live in and work to make some changes that overall will be good for the town."

An involuntary blush crawled up my neck; I was actually touched by Kyran's words. It was very nice of him to say, and I only hoped that my plan could live up to expectations.

"So you can get me a projector and a DVD?"

"Sure," Kyran said. "I assume you're going to take care of having a screen ready?"

I nodded. "I'm pretty sure Amy can make a big white screen out of nothing with her magic."

"What movie did you want me to get?"

"Have you ever heard of *Spice World*?" A part of me really hoped he hadn't. As much as I enjoyed that movie, it was basically the girliest, most immature thing on the planet.

The look Kyran gave me, on the other hand, told me that he was very well aware of what *Spice World* entailed.

"You mean the movie that features award-winning actor Richard E. Grant?"

"Yes, that one."

"Of course I can get that for you," Kyran laughed. "Although I'm curious as to how you came to the conclusion that that would be a good first choice instead of one of the major classics, like, you know, *Star Wars*."

"It's possible someone asked me what movie I was showing, and I panicked and said *Spice World*, and now I can't back out of it," I admitted, and Kyran laughed.

"Well, there certainly are worse movies out there. I'll get you everything you need, and bring it by your place tomorrow morning if that works for you."

"Thank you so much," I said, a grin crossing my face. My heart swelled as I realized my plan was actually coming together, and I might actually pull this off after all.

"Not a problem. It's for a good cause, I'm happy to help. I'll see you tomorrow."

As Kyran made his way back towards The White Tree, Mr. Meowgi and I walked back home.

"Well, that was far less of an adventure than I had been hoping for," Mr. Meowgi complained.

"Hey, they can't all be super exciting," I said. "Besides, you never know what's going to happen at my party tomorrow. Although honestly, I'd be very okay with it if it ended up being the most boring party ever and nothing interesting happened."

"It certainly sounds like it's going to be boring," Mr. Meowgi said. "You should have asked me what movie you were going to play; I'd have said *The Karate Kid* in a heartbeat."

"Well, if it goes well and this becomes a regular thing, then you'll probably get your wish eventually," I said with a wink.

I really, really hoped this went well. While a part of me was excited, a part of me was also a little bit scared. After all, I was still very new in town, and I wasn't sure that throwing myself out there and making a huge mark in the community straight away was the best idea.

Still, it was too late to turn back now. I was dedicated, and I was going to do my best to do this right.

CHAPTER 21

*A*s soon as I got home, I found Amy, Sara, and Ellie in the living room, all of them looking intently at the TV.

I had never really gotten a good look at a paranormal TV; up until now I had kind of assumed that it was exactly the same as a regular human TV. However, the screen had grown to take up almost the entire wall of the room, and everything was three-dimensional; it was more like watching a play than watching a screen.

"What's going on?" I asked as I tried to make sense of the scene in front of me. It looked like a shot from in front of Hexpresso Bean. In fact, I was almost certain that was where it was from.

"Chief Enforcer King is arresting Farawir," Amy said in a hushed whisper. I turned the screen to watch. Sure enough, while it wasn't super noticeable because the camera was so far away, Chief Enforcer King's blonde hair stood out anyway. She was leading away an elf who looked suspiciously like Farawir as others looked on. A minute later, the camera turned to a fairy with a blond bob and gold glasses that matched her wings.

"We have just seen the startling images of the elf Farawir, son of recently murdered community stalwart Lorondir, being arrested for the murder of his father. This is happening live, right in downtown Western Woods. I'm going to make my way towards Chief Enforcer King to see if she has any more information."

I turned to Sara. "This is great news for you, at least. Now you can go back to your job, right?"

"I hope so," Sara said, allowing herself the glimpse of a smile. "I actually did enjoy the job. It was nice, being able to use my broom for something."

"You really should thank Amy for this," I said. "It's all because she was studying law in the coven library that this happened at all."

Ellie gave me a strange look. "There are no books about law in the coven library; that's not something witches study at all."

I looked over at Amy, and noticed the blush creeping up the back of her neck. I grinned.

"You snuck into the elf library to study law, didn't you?"

The other two girls gasped, as if this was the most surprising thing they had ever heard in their lives.

"Did you really?" Sara asked, her mouth agape.

"I knew she wanted to be a lawyer!" Ellie shouted triumphantly. "And I also knew she had a bit of a rebellious streak in her."

Amy scowled. "Fine, so I don't think that education should be limited to a certain species. Is that so much to ask?"

I grinned. Amy was definitely starting to come around. And now, with the murder of Lorondir solved, I could focus on the party.

"I organized the movie for tomorrow," I said. "We're going to be watching *Spice World*."

"Ooh, is that a movie about the spice islands in the East?" Amy asked, and I shot her a look.

"First of all, I don't think anybody has called them the spice islands in like three hundred years, at least, and secondly no, it's a movie about pop stars in England."

"Oh," Amy said, looking a little bit dejected. Ellie laughed.

"I think it sounds awesome," she said. "I'll make some extra cinnamon buns at work tomorrow and bring them along. You have any idea how many people are going to come?"

I shook my head. "I have no idea. The vampires will know about it, but whether or not anybody will show up is a whole different story. We'll see. I'm not getting my hopes up; honestly I'd be really happy if there were like, ten people there."

Sara nodded. "Good idea, keep your expectations

low, just in case. Besides, no matter what, we are going to be there, and I know we're going to have fun."

"Thanks," I said to my friends. I was really glad that no matter what, I knew I could always count on them.

≈

*T*he next morning Amy was gone somewhere - probably the library - by the time I had woken up, Ellie was at her job at Hexpresso Bean, and Sara left me a note that she had gone back to the law firm to see if she was rehired now that Farawir had been arrested for the murder and she was no longer a suspect.

I poured myself a bowl of cereal and tried to quell the nerves that were building up inside of me despite everything. After a while, there was a knock at the door, and Kyran came by with a large projector, a DVD player, a copy of *Spice World* on DVD, and instructions on how to use all of it.

"This is awesome," I said with a grin as I connected everything in the living room and shone the projector onto the wall. "Thank you so much."

"Don't mention it," Kyran said, shaking his head. "This is for a good cause."

"Are you going to come tonight?"

Kyran shook his head. "Believe me, if I thought that it would in any way improve things, I would be there.

But I think given my position in this society, an appearance by me can only harm your cause."

Disappointment welled up inside of me, despite everything. "That's too bad," I said. "I would have liked for you to be there."

"Well, maybe one day things will get good enough that I'll be able to show my face in public without everyone looking at me with scorn and ridicule. But, we're not quite there yet."

"If you're sure, then," I said, trying to hide the disappointment in my voice.

"Trust me, it's for the best. I hope it goes off really well for you, I'll be cheering for you."

"Thanks," I said with a smile. After Kyran left I familiarized myself with the projector even further and started to really get ready for my event that night.

By the time 8 o'clock rolled around, I was a mess. I hadn't organized an event well, ever, and I had absolutely underestimated how much work was going to go into it. Luckily, magic made things a lot easier.

Amy came back home at around five and went down to the gardens with me; Sara followed after us with all of the movie equipment, and the two of us got started while Ellie stayed at home to take care of the last of the food and drinks.

"Are you going to have chairs?" Amy asked as we made our way to a large clearing in the garden. I figured this was a nice place to have the movie; the lake was just to the left of the clearing which gave a great view over the rest of the park while leaving plenty of space in case by some miracle half the town showed up.

"I don't know," I said, my heart sinking. I hadn't even thought of chairs. How on earth was I going to get dozens of them ready now? "I guess chairs would be good; or maybe I could try to find some blankets last second so people could just sit down on the grass?"

Amy pointed to the grass and a couple of seconds later about a dozen extra-large picnic blankets appeared out of nowhere. She moved her wand a little bit and a dozen lawn chairs suddenly manifested themselves on the lawn as well.

"There. Now you have both: anyone who wants to sit down on the grass can do so, and if you have some older people who would rather sit on a chair, then they're covered as well."

I looked at Amy, gratitude written all over my face. "Thank you so much," I said. "I don't even know what I would do without you."

"Well, you wouldn't have a screen to project the movie onto, either," Amy laughed, pointing her wand to the clearing and making a huge, white screen appear out of nowhere as well. I shook my head, incredulous.

"That's amazing."

"If you continue your studies, and if we eventually discover which coven you belong to, there's no reason why you won't be able to do this as well."

I nodded, but the idea still seemed so far out into the future that it didn't seem real. I was still working on learning really basic spells; making stuff appear out of nowhere definitely didn't seem like it was going to happen anytime soon.

"This is set up as well," Sara said, motioning towards the projector. "Ellie just texted, she's coming over now with all the food."

Everything was really coming together.

An hour later, as the sun was really setting and we were definitely in the twilight period, I started to get a little bit antsy. After all, I had told the other girls to let people know to get here after the sunset, and I really hoped that at least a few people would show up.

"It's going to be fine, people will come," Amy said.

"We told a lot of people," Ellie said. "Trust me, a few will show up."

I was just starting to lose hope as dusk turned into a true night and Amy set up some fairy lights around the space. No one was coming after all.

Then, out of nowhere, I began to hear the sound of voices. I looked to see where they were coming from, and found Bluebell, one of the fairies who worked at Hexpresso Bean, making her way over with four other fairies in tow. One of them was Aurora, one of the other fairies who worked at the coffee shop, but I didn't recognize the other two.

"Tina, thank you so much for doing this," Bluebell said, as she and her crew made her way over to me.

"Of course," I smiled. "I thought it would be really fun for everyone to watch a human movie."

"I've never seen one," one of the other fairies said, her red wings fluttering excitedly behind her. "I'm very excited."

Just then, Maria Grecu, the vampire who was currently on trial for biting people, came out of the woods as well. She looked a little bit nervous, and when she saw that there were no other vampires around it looked like she was going to turn and walk away, but Ellie quickly made her way towards her and assured her that she was totally welcome.

It looked like we weren't going to have zero turnout after all.

After I made sure that the fairies were nicely settled on some of the picnic blankets, I turned to find Jackson Lupo, the head of the shifters, standing on the edge of the woods, and my heart skipped a beat. Jackson was tall, blonde, and every bit the strong lion shifter. He strode towards me with confidence, a smile on his face.

"When I heard the new witch in town was having a party, I figured I had to come by and make an appearance," he told me.

"Thanks for coming," I stammered. "I hope you like the movie."

"I think you'll find that my taste in movies is very broad," Jackson said with a smile. "I think a few others from my tribe are coming along as well."

Before I knew it, there were thirty people all milling around. Sure, no one was mingling with one another – the fairies were speaking with the fairies, Maria had found a second vampire who had shown up, and that sort of thing – but the point was, everyone was here together for now.

Even a few elves had shown up – Manarwa, from the law firm, was here with Lorondir's sister Elawa.

"Alright, everyone, we're going to get going in a few minutes, if everyone wants to find a seat," Ellie called out to the crowd. Slowly but surely, all of the paranormals made their way to the seats in front of the projector, and I moved in front of the screen. After all, I figured that at the very least I should say a few words before the movie started.

"Hey everyone," I started. "I wanted to thank you all for coming to my movie night. As most of you know, I'm definitely new in town, and I'm from the human world where we have a bunch of great movies that apparently none of you have ever seen. So, I figured I would fix that by having movie nights here in the coven gardens every so often and I wanted to thank you all for coming. I hope you'll enjoy the movie."

I motioned to Sara, who was standing behind the projector, and she started playing the film.

CHAPTER 22

To my surprise, absolutely everybody seemed to love *Spice World.* Raucous laughter poured from the crowd appropriately, and I had to admit, I was very much enjoying this movie as well. It had been quite a few years since I had last seen it, and despite the fact that it was *very* 90s, it held up surprisingly well for being a twenty-year-old movie.

The movie definitely had its intended effect: when it had finished, all of the paranormals made their way towards the table where Ellie had left out all of the food, and to my immense joy, I couldn't help but notice that the different paranormals were even speaking to one another.

"I loved the bit where they all fell out of the boat," Bluebell said to one of the other fairies.

"That was absolutely my favorite bit as well," Maria

Grecu said, and the fairies all moved to let her into the circle.

"Posh Spice being angry about her dress being dry cleaned only was phenomenal," Bluebell said. This was really happening; the movie had broken the ice between all of the paranormals, and they were now interacting normally instead of adhering to the super strict hierarchy that seemed to dominate life here in Western Woods.

Maybe there was hope yet; maybe my plan was actually going to work. Sure, I wasn't going to change paranormal minds overnight; one night with the Spice Girls, as awesome as it was, wasn't going to be enough to destroy a hierarchy that had existed for thousands of years, but slowly, I was going to chip away at this outdated ideal that the different species of paranormals were too different from one another to truly be integrated together.

I noticed a rustling in the woods, and suddenly Kyran appeared from behind a tree. He had been here after all. I smiled and grinned, but he simply held up a finger to his lips, winked, and turned away. He wasn't going to make a public appearance, but he had been here, and that made me happy.

"I'm going to head home," Sara said a few minutes later, coming towards me. I had just finished having a conversation with Manarwa and Lorondir's sister, Elawa, thanking them for coming. They had told me that while the movie wasn't their usual style, they had very much enjoyed it. "After all, it turns out that I might have another job lined up on top of the one at the law firm."

"Really?" I asked, a smile crossing my face. Everything was coming up Sara right now, and I didn't know anyone who deserved it more.

"Yeah," she replied. "I got my old job back at the law firm, but I was at the post office this morning dropping off some papers for one of the lawyers, and I spoke to the lady there who told me that they could use someone like me for emergencies."

"Emergencies?"

"Yeah, like when all the owls are out of commission for a few days because there's an illness, like what happened earlier this week."

Right. The post office owls. I made a mental note to make my way over there; I wanted to see just how similar to Harry Potter it really was.

"That's great news," I said to Sara. "Thanks so much for all the help tonight. We'll have to go out and celebrate at some point when all four of us have an evening off."

"Oh, it's nothing that good," Sara said, a blush rising up her face. I had a feeling Sara really wasn't used to getting praised all that much. I made my way over to her and gave her a hug.

"I'm super proud of you; I'm so glad you're finding your place in this world."

When I pulled away, I couldn't help but notice

Sara's eyes glimmering in the glow of the lights Amy had put up, and I realized just how affected she was by my words.

"I'll see you tomorrow," she said with a wave before heading on back home.

All of a sudden, a chill ran through my spine. Everything made sense, and I realized that Farawir hadn't killed Lorondir.

I had to find Chief Enforcer King, and I had to find her now.

I made my way over to Ellie, who I knew had the day off the next day. "Hey, sorry to bail like this but you mind taking care of everything for a little bit? I swear, it's super important."

"Sure," Ellie said with a nod. "Do what you need to do."

"Thanks, I owe you one," I said, running off in the direction of town. After all, Chief Enforcer King would most likely be at her office at this time of night, right? Well, okay, she was probably home, but someone at her office would be the best way for me to find out where she lived.

As I raced through the forest, I suddenly heard a voice calling out behind me.

"Tina, excuse me, Tina."

I stopped to see who was calling after me, and as soon as I did, my blood ran cold. It was Elawa, the very person I was about to go tell Chief Enforcer King was a murderer.

"Hi, Elawa. What can I do for you?" Elves had a real intuition-based magic, and I did my best to not think of her as a murderer, and to keep my thoughts light and airy. After all, while elves couldn't read thoughts directly, they could definitely feel a person's energy.

"I couldn't help but notice you running off," Elawa said. "Is everything alright?"

"Of course," I said with what I hoped looked like an easy smile. "I just remembered that I forgot something at home, and so the other girls are taking care of cleaning up for me."

"I see. So it didn't have anything to do with that conversation you just had with your friend?"

"What conversation?" I asked with a tilt my head.

"About the owls at the post office."

My blood ran cold and I swallowed hard. Elawa had overheard the conversation, and she must have thought that I ran off because I had finally pieced everything together. She was definitely right, and now here I was, alone with a murderer away from anywhere else.

"Oh, that conversation was nothing," I said, trying to wave it off as a regular thing. "I simply didn't realize that the post office here uses owls, and I think that's pretty cool."

"I know it's more than that," Elawa said. "I felt that pulsating energy as soon as you connected everything. You know that I wasn't told that I was no longer in my brother's will."

Great. The game was up. I nodded. "Yeah, I did only

just figure it out then. And then it made sense. You found out that he had sold his shares of the partnership, and that he had just gotten a huge payday, and you killed him, thinking that you were going to be the beneficiary in his will. But you never got the notification that the will had been changed, because the post office owls had all come down with the same infection that prevented them from flying."

"Stupid owls," Elawa said. "And stupid Lorondir. His son is a worthless piece of trash with a gambling addiction, who's just going to waste away his inheritance. I deserve that money. I'm the one who spent my whole life looking after Lorondir, making sure he always had meals, while he went off being this super famous lawyer making all this money. I deserved that inheritance."

"So you killed him for it, and you're not even getting any money for it."

Elawa barked out a laugh. "We'll see. I'm patient. It's one of the advantages of being over 2000 years old. That idiot Farawir won't have a will made, so I just need to wait a few years and kill him off as well; the money will go to me and my brother, his closest living relatives."

"Not if you go to jail for Lorondir's murder first," I said.

"And who's going to tell Chief Enforcer King? I know you are on your way to see her, and that's why I came to stop you. And trust me. I'm going to stop you."

I instinctively reached into the back pocket of my pants and began fingering my wand. Maybe I was finally turning into a witch after all; magic was instinctively what I was turning to. Except, the problem was, I still knew very few spells, and the ones I did know weren't going to be especially helpful here.

Elawa took a step towards me, and my heart pounded in my chest.

"That's right, you should be scared," Elawa said with a nasty grin. "I'm going to make sure you regret ever coming to Western Woods and meddling your little nose into my affairs."

I looked around. We were still in the coven gardens, and there was no one in sight. The lake was to my left and a few large trees were scattered here and there, but there was nothing that I could see that could help me make an escape.

Maybe if I ran to the lake, I could manage to get there before Elawa did? Then I could swim away. But what if elves could swim? Elawa was a lot taller than me, and had longer limbs. If she could swim in the water as well, then that wouldn't help me at all.

Before I had a chance to make a final decision, however, Elawa held out a hand and the ground underneath me began to tremble. I ran to my right just as the ground opened up into a giant hole, with me scrambling away from the edge as fast as I could. Elawa was not playing around; I had to do something before I ended up dead.

"Jupiter, bring forth fire, the cousin of Lightning," I shouted, pointing my wand at Elawa and focusing all of my energy on the spell. A small flame shot out from my wand and towards the elf, but it wasn't powerful enough to reach her, and Elawa laughed as she looked at the results of my spell.

"I can't believe you think you're a match against me," she said. "I have thousands of years of experience with elfin magic, and you're trying spells that a six-year-old could master and failing."

I narrowed my eyes at her. Honestly, the words didn't hurt one bit. After all, I might've been a terrible witch, but at least I wasn't a murderer. Still, if I was going to get out of here alive, I was going to have to figure out a way to do this spell more powerfully.

Elawa reached her hands out towards me again, and once again as the ground beneath me trembled, I scrambled away as once more the earth fell away and a large pit developed. I knew that if I ended up inside one of those pits, it was all over for me.

"Why don't you just let this happen? You're only delaying the inevitable," Elawa snarled at me as I ran from side to side. Suddenly, I realized that she was so transfixed on me, that Elawa wasn't paying too much attention to what else was going on around her. I ran from side to side as she continued to make the pits, trying not to make it obvious what I was doing, but eventually, I managed to essentially isolate Elawa on an island, as she had opened pits up all around herself in an attempt to trap me.

I stopped, and laughed.

"What is it?" she said. "Why are you laughing?"

Instead of answering, I replied with a spell. But this time, instead of pointing my wand at Elawa herself, I pointed it at the grass on the little makeshift island she was now standing on.

"*Jupiter, bring forth fire, the cousin of Lightning,*" I tried again, and this time, the flame caught on the grass and it began to smolder.

"What are you doing? Get away!" Elawa shouted as she began to try and stamp out the fire. That distraction was what I needed to get people's attention. After all, I needed someone else here to help.

Running over to the nearest large tree, I did the spell once more, pointed my wand at one of the smaller branches covered with leaves.

"Sorry, mister tree," I whispered to the tree as the leaves and branch caught fire, and the tree began to burn. I really, really hoped that someone would eventually notice and come by to help.

To my surprise, no matter how much Elawa was stamping out the flames on the grass, it didn't seem to matter. The fire stayed lit, and eventually the edge of her robes caught, and fire engulfed her.

"Help me!" she began to screech as the flames enveloped her body.

I gasped; I had wanted to distract Elawa, not immolate her. As her screams filled the night, I did what I knew I had to: I took my wand, and I did another spell.

"Jupiter, God of thunder, use my wand and bring forth water."

I repeated the spell three or four times, every time resulting in water gushing forth from my wand, until finally the flames were out and Elawa lay on the ground in a crumpled heap.

I didn't know what to do, so I just kind of stared in horror, hoping that despite everything Elawa wasn't dead. After all, she might have been a murderer, but I wanted her to face justice for her crimes. And I didn't want to be a murderer. I hadn't meant to kill her; I had only wanted to distract her.

"Tina? What's going on?" I heard Ellie ask behind me. I turned to find her, Sara and Amy rushing towards me.

"I don't know if she's dead or not," was all I could say, pointing at the elf still crumbled in a heap.

"I'll go get my mom," Sara said, rushing back from where she came, obviously to get her broom so she could fly the hospital.

Elawa groaned suddenly and began to move. At least it meant she wasn't dead.

"She's the one who killed Lorondir," I said. "She tried to kill me, and I tried to distract her and accidentally set her on fire."

"Don't move," Amy said to Elawa, taking out her wand and pointing it at the elf.

"Help me," Elawa begged.

"Healers are on their way, but don't you dare move," Amy said. "Trust me, if you try to hurt Tina again I will destroy you."

At Amy's words, the reality of the situation rushed over me, and I collapsed onto the ground, completely overrun by emotion and exhaustion.

Ten minutes later, Sara's mom Heather, three elf Healers and two elf assistants came over, the assistants carrying a number of medical supplies. Amy did a quick spell to fill in the pits that Elawa had created, and the medical staff quickly made their way over to her as she moaned in pain.

Ellie had gone over to find Chief Enforcer King, and texted us to let us know that King would meet us at the hospital, where she wanted to take our statements before arresting Elawa.

"I thought you weren't going to get involved with this," Chief Enforcer King told me with a serious expression on her face as soon as she saw me.

"I genuinely wasn't," I replied earnestly. And it was true; I had gone to do the right thing, but Elawa had eavesdropped and realized what I knew. "I was on my way to get you, when Elawa stopped me."

"How did you know it was her?"

"It was the owls. Amy's familiar is an owl, and she mentioned that all of the owls in town got an infection that stopped them from flying for the past week. So, when we uh, may have noticed that a copy of the new will was sent to Elawa on Monday, it didn't click then, but there was no way she could have gotten the mail. After all, all of the owls were sick, so they weren't doing deliveries."

"How did you know that Lorondir had seen his sister that morning? Did she have the opportunity to poison him?"

"It didn't click at the time, but one of the fairies told me that Lorondir and his sister had coffee together every Wednesday morning. Lorondir was murdered on Wednesday, so she would have met with him that morning for coffee."

Chief Enforcer King nodded. "I have to admit, I am impressed that a witch managed to figure all of this out."

I grinned. "Does that mean I'm not in trouble?"

"Only because your friends back up your statement that you left to go and find me, and that you were followed and attacked. However, in the future, I would appreciate it if you did your best to stay out of trouble."

"Don't worry," I replied with a small smile. "I have absolutely no intention of getting into any more trouble."

"Good." Chief Enforcer King closed her notebook.

"Elawa isn't admitting to anything, but I think we have plenty of evidence here to put her way for life. I think as soon as she gets in touch with a lawyer - it's too bad for her she killed the best criminal lawyer in town - she might change her tune when she sees how much jail time she's about to face."

I said goodbye to Chief Enforcer King, and a few minutes later my friends all came over to see me.

"How did you know that it was Elawa who did it?" Amy asked, curiosity written all over her face. I explained everything that I had figured out to the three of them, and Amy groaned.

"I should've figured that out," she said. "After all, Kevin is my familiar, and I knew that the owls were all sick."

Ellie grinned. "Poor Amy. It must be so hard for her when someone else solves the puzzle first. You know, Amy, you would probably make a pretty good enforcer."

"Please," Amy scoffed. "I'm a witch. I can't be an enforcer."

Ellie winked at me, and I smiled back. After all, the first movie night had gone better than I could've expected - well, other than that whole part where I was almost killed by a murderer. But I was confident that given time, I could change the attitudes of the people here in Western Woods and make them realize that they weren't all that different from one another after all.

First of all, I wanted to thank you for reading this book. I well and truly hope you enjoyed reading this book as much as I loved writing it.

If you enjoyed Two Peas in a Potion I'd really appreciate it if you could take a moment and leave a review for the book on Amazon, to help other readers find the book as well.

Want to read more of Tina's adventures? The third book in the Western Woods Mystery series is now available.

Other Western Woods Mysteries

Back to Spell One (Western Woods Mystery #1)

Three's a Coven (Western Woods Mystery #3)

Four Leaf Clovers (Western Woods Mystery #4)

Willow Bay Witches Mysteries

The Purr-fect Crime (Willow Bay Witches #1)

Barking up the Wrong Tree (Willow Bay Witches #2)

Just Horsing Around (Willow Bay Witches #3)

Lipstick on a Pig (Willow Bay Witches #4)

A Grizzly Discovery (Willow Bay Witches #5)

Sleeping with the Fishes (Willow Bay Witches #6)

Get your Ducks in a Row (Willow Bay Witches #7)

Busy as a Beaver (Willow Bay Witches #8)

Magical Bookshop Mysteries

Alice in Murderland (Magical Bookshop Mystery #1)

Murder on the Oregon Express (Magical Bookshop Mystery #2)

The Very Killer Caterpillar (Magical Bookshop Mystery #3)

Death Quixote (Magical Bookshop Mystery #4)

Pride and Premeditation (Magical Bookshop Mystery #5)

Moonlight Cove Mysteries

Witching Aint's Easy (Moonlight Cove Mystery #1)

Witching for the Best (Moonlight Cove Mystery #2)

Thank your Lucky Spells (Moonlight Cove Mystery #3)

A Perfect Spell (Moonlight Cove Mystery #4)

California Witching Mysteries

Witches and Wine (California Witching Mystery #1)

Poison and Pinot (California Witching Mystery #2)

Merlot and Murder (California Witching Mystery #3)

Cassie Coburn Mysteries

Poison in Paddington (Cassie Coburn Mystery #1)

Bombing in Belgravia (Cassie Coburn Mystery #2)

Whacked in Whitechapel (Cassie Coburn Mystery #3)

Strangled in Soho (Cassie Coburn Mystery #4)

Stabbed in Shoreditch (Cassie Coburn Mystery #5)

Killed in King's Cross (Cassie Coburn Mystery #6)

Ruby Bay Mysteries

Death Down Under (Ruby Bay Mystery #1)

Arson in Australia (Ruby Bay Mystery #2)

The Killer Kangaroo (Ruby Bay Mystery #3)

ABOUT THE AUTHOR

Samantha Silver lives in British Columbia, Canada, along with her husband and a little old doggie named Terra. She loves animals, skiing and of course, writing cozy mysteries.

You can connect with Samantha online on Facebook.

Printed in Great Britain
by Amazon